W9-CBJ-059

"Four Eyes" and No Friends?

Elizabeth opened the door. Jessica was lying on her bed with her face buried in a pillow. Slowly, she turned her head to look at Elizabeth. Her face was red and splotchy from crying.

"Jessica," Elizabeth said gently, joining her on the bed, "don't you think you're overreacting a little?"

Jessica sniffed loudly. "That's easy for you to say. You won't have to look like the biggest nerd in the universe." She rolled over onto her back. "Elizabeth, what will Aaron think if I show up at school on Tuesday wearing glasses?"

"If he stops liking you just because you're wearing glasses, then he's not worth your time to begin with," Elizabeth said logically.

"But I . . . I really like Aaron, Elizabeth."

Bantam Skylark Books in the SWEET VALLEY TWINS AND FRIENDS® series.
Ask your bookseller for the books you have missed.

SWEET VALLEY TWINS
AND FRIENDS

Jessica's New Look

Written by
Jamie Suzanne

Created by
FRANCINE PASCAL

A BANTAM SKYLARK BOOK
NEW YORK · TORONTO · LONDON · SYDNEY · AUCKLAND

RL4, 008–012

JESSICA'S NEW LOOK
A Bantam Skylark Book / April 1991

*Sweet Valley High and Sweet Valley Twins and Friends are registered
trademarks of Francine Pascal*

Conceived by Francine Pascal

*Produced by Daniel Weiss Associates, Inc.
33 West 17th Street
New York, NY 10011*

Cover art by James Mathewuse

*Skylark Books is a registered trademark of Bantam Books, a division of
Bantam Doubleday Dell Publishing Group, Inc.
Registered in U.S. Patent and Trademark Office and elsewhere.*

*All rights reserved.
Copyright © 1991 by Francine Pascal.
No part of this book may be reproduced or transmitted in any form or by
any means, electronic or mechanical, including photocopying, recording,
or by any information storage and retrieval system, without permission in
writing from the publisher.
For information address: Bantam Books.*

*If you purchased this book without a cover you should be aware that
this book is stolen property. It was reported as "unsold and destroyed"
to the publisher and neither the author nor the publisher has received
any payment for this "stripped book."*

ISBN 0-553-15869-4

Published simultaneously in the United States and Canada

*Bantam Books are published by Bantam Books, a division of Bantam Double-
day Dell Publishing Group, Inc. Its trademark, consisting of the words
"Bantam Books" and the portrayal of a rooster, is Registered in U.S. Patent
and Trademark Office and in other countries. Marca Registrada. Bantam
Books, 1540 Broadway, New York, New York 10036.*

PRINTED IN THE UNITED STATES OF AMERICA

OPM   15 14 13 12 11 10 9 8 7

One

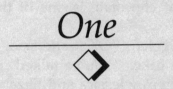

"Mind if I cut in?"

Jessica Wakefield eased into the lunch line behind her twin sister, Elizabeth, on Wednesday afternoon. She flashed a brilliant smile at the boy she'd just cut in front of, and he smiled back shyly.

"Jess, you really should go to the end of the line and wait your turn," Elizabeth said. She reached for an apple and placed it on her lunch tray.

"But I've already been through once," Jessica protested. "All I want now is a piece of cake." She glanced down at Elizabeth's tray and made a face. "What *are* those green things, anyway?"

"Brussels sprouts," Elizabeth replied. "They're good for you."

Jessica shook her head and carefully scanned the display of desserts. She chose a large slice of chocolate cake and placed it on Elizabeth's lunch tray. "So is chocolate," she said. "Didn't we learn in science that chocolate is one of the four basic food groups?"

Elizabeth giggled. "OK," she said, reaching for a piece of the cake. "You've talked me into it!"

Anyone who saw Jessica and Elizabeth standing next to each other would have trouble telling them apart. The girls were identical twins. They both had long, sun-streaked blond hair, bright blue-green eyes, and a tiny dimple in the left cheek.

But no matter how much they looked alike, their personalities were very different. Elizabeth was a few minutes older and the more serious, conscientious twin. She dreamed of becoming a journalist some day and devoted much of her time and energy to the *Sweet Valley Sixers*, the sixth-grade newspaper that she had helped found. Elizabeth was usually very logical and sensible, and always loyal and kind. Her friends knew she could always be counted on to help out with any problem they might have.

Jessica could be counted on, too—to have a good time, no matter what she was up to! She was a member of the exclusive Unicorn Club, a group of the most popular girls at Sweet Valley Middle School. The Unicorns liked to think of themselves as the royalty of Sweet Valley Middle School, and because purple is the color of royalty, each Unicorn tried to wear something purple every day. Like all the Unicorns, Jessica loved talking about clothes and boys, topics she found much more interesting than anything Elizabeth ever published in the pages of the *Sixers*.

When they were younger, Elizabeth and Jessica had dressed alike and shared the same friends. Now the two girls had very different styles and completely different friends and interests. But nothing would ever change the fact that they had a special bond that only twins could share.

"I meant to tell you, Jess," Elizabeth said as they headed toward the cashier. "I won't be able to walk home with you today. Mr. Bowman asked to see me after school." Mr. Bowman, who taught sixth-grade English, was also the faculty supervisor for the *Sixers*. "He said he had something important to discuss with me."

"Uh-oh." Jessica shook her head. "Any time a teacher asks a student to stay after school, it's bad news, even for you, Elizabeth!" she teased. "I've got an emergency Boosters practice after school, so I couldn't have walked home with you anyway."

"Emergency?" Elizabeth echoed with a smile. The Boosters was a cheering squad organized by the Unicorns. "What exactly *is* a Boosters emergency, anyway?"

"At our last practice we kept dropping our batons. One even bounced off Coach Cassels's head as he was walking by," Jessica said.

"Was he hurt?" Elizabeth asked.

"No, but he definitely didn't think it was very funny."

"Whose baton was it?" Elizabeth wanted to know.

Jessica's cheeks turned pink, but she lifted her chin. "Mine. But I had a good reason for being distracted. Aaron Dallas had just walked by and smiled at me."

"Oh." Elizabeth tried not to smile. "That explains everything."

"Aaron Dallas is probably the cutest guy in the entire sixth grade, Elizabeth. You just don't ignore it when someone like Aaron *smiles* at you."

Elizabeth paused in front of the cashier, who looked at her tray and laughed. "Two pieces of cake?" the woman remarked. "You must be awfully hungry."

"Elizabeth's a very big eater," Jessica explained with mock seriousness.

Elizabeth rolled her eyes and paid for the food. "You owe me seventy-five cents for the cake," she told her twin.

But Jessica didn't seem to have heard her. "Look!" she whispered excitedly. She pointed across the lunchroom toward the Unicorner, the table where the Unicorns gathered at lunchtime. "There are *boys* sitting at the Unicorner!"

"So?" Elizabeth shrugged.

"*So*? When was the last time *you* had lunch with Bruce Patman? Or Jake Hamilton? Or—" Jessica paused, squinting at the table. "Who's that other guy?"

"Aaron Dallas," Elizabeth answered matter-of-factly. "Don't you even recognize him? I thought he was supposed to be so cute!"

"I *recognize* him," Jessica replied in annoyance. "I just couldn't see him very well. He *is* across the room, you know." Jessica smoothed her hair. "See you, Elizabeth."

"Don't you want your cake?" Elizabeth called.

"You can have it. After all, you *are* a big eater," Jessica added mischievously.

She hurried toward the Unicorner. Jake, Aaron, and Bruce were sitting at one end of the table. She couldn't believe that they were actually eating lunch with the Unicorns, at the Unicorner! Normally, the boys sat at the opposite end of the lunchroom.

"Hi, everyone!" Jessica said brightly as she approached the table.

All three boys looked up at Jessica and smiled. "Hi, Jessica," Aaron said shyly.

"Where's your cake?" Lila Fowler demanded. Lila was a sixth-grade Unicorn and one of Jessica's closest friends.

"What cake? You know I don't eat cake. Cake makes you fat." Jessica beamed at the three boys. "Mind if I sit down?"

"There's a chair down here," Ellen Riteman informed Jessica from the other end of the table, farthest from the boys.

"That's OK," Jessica said. "I'll just sit here, next to Aaron."

As she slid into her seat, Jessica noticed the other Unicorns giving her some nasty looks, but she didn't care. She was sitting next to three of the cutest boys in the school, and she was certain that all the eyes in the lunchroom were on her.

Jessica cleared her throat. It seemed that all of a sudden everyone at the table had grown very quiet. "So," she began, "what brings you guys to the Unicorner?"

"We were hoping you'd make us honorary

members," Bruce joked. Bruce was a seventh grader, and he came from one of the richest families in town. The Unicorns thought he was adorable.

"And besides, there was nowhere else to sit," Jake added.

"Maybe we *could* make you honorary Unicorns," Lila suggested. "You could even come to our meetings. Of course, you'd have to wear something purple every day."

"Give me a break, Fowler!" Bruce snorted.

"I think we'll pass on that one," Aaron added, smiling at Jessica. Aaron was one of the tallest sixth graders. Jessica especially liked his dark brown eyes.

Again the group fell silent, which Jessica thought was strange. The Unicorns *always* had something to talk about. Jessica noticed another strange thing. Although their lunch trays were piled high with food, all the girls seemed to have stopped eating. Only the three boys seemed to be interested in their lunch.

"What did you think of that pop quiz in math, Bruce?" asked Kimberly Haver, a seventh-grade Unicorn.

Bruce had just taken a big bite out of his hamburger. "I don't know," he mumbled, his mouth full of food. He paused to swallow. "Why would anyone ever need to multiply fractions, anyway?"

Kimberly laughed a bit too loudly. "You're absolutely right. I'm sure I flunked," she said, fluttering her dark lashes.

"Is there something in your eye, Kimberly?" Jessica asked politely.

Kimberly shot her a withering look. The table was quiet again. The three boys were completely absorbed in their food.

Jessica shifted uncomfortably in her chair. She'd imagined that having boys at the Unicorner would have been more entertaining. What was it boys liked to talk about, anyway? She thought of her fourteen-year-old brother, Steven. What did he like? Food, of course. But Aaron, Bruce, and Jake were probably more interested in eating than in talking about food. Steven also liked basketball.

That was it! The three boys played basketball for Sweet Valley Middle School.

Jessica turned to Aaron. "I saw you guys at basketball practice the other day. The team looks great."

Aaron grinned widely. "We've got some work to do on our defense, but Coach Cassels says we have a real chance at a winning season."

Jessica nodded. "My brother Steven plays on the Sweet Valley High team."

"He's good, too," Jake said. "I saw him play against Johnson High."

"Well, anyway, Steven says that a team's only as strong as its defense." Jessica kept her eyes fixed on Aaron.

"He's right!" Aaron agreed.

From her seat at the other end of the table, Lila yawned, making a show of patting her mouth with her hand. "Did anyone see that movie on TV last night?"

"*Broken Hearts*?" Mary Wallace asked. "I cried through the whole thing!"

"Did you see it, Bruce?" Lila leaned toward him and cupped her hand in her chin.

Bruce shook his head. "I watched the Celtics and the Lakers game on the all-sports cable channel."

"That was a great game!" Jessica said enthusiastically. "I watched the second half with my brother."

Lila tossed her light-brown hair over her shoulder. "The Lakers are an incredible baseball team," she agreed, still focusing all her attention on Bruce.

"Baseball?" Bruce rolled his eyes. "The Lakers play *basketball*!"

Lila's face turned bright red, and the rest of the

group laughed. "I knew that," she shot back haughtily. "I was just kidding around."

"They would have won if it wasn't for that blocking penalty in the last two minutes of the game," Aaron said.

Bruce shook his head. "That was a bad call. He was just playing good, aggressive defense."

"No, it was a good call," Jessica disagreed.

All eyes turned toward her. Bruce frowned skeptically. "What do *you* know about it, blondie? I'll bet you don't even know what blocking is!"

"It's when a defensive player moves into the path of an offensive player and interferes with his movement," Jessica answered nonchalantly.

"Oh, yeah?" Bruce sounded somewhat taken aback. "That's just good defense."

Jessica shook her head. "The defensive player has to be set up, facing the offensive player with both his feet on the floor, before the offensive player runs into him. If he isn't set up, it's blocking. If he's set up and the offensive player plows into him, then it's a charging penalty against the offense."

"Could you repeat that?" Ellen asked, looking totally confused. "In English?"

Bruce whistled in amazement. "Did your big brother teach you that stuff?"

"Actually, Bruce, although you boys don't like

to admit it, there *is* a girl's basketball team, and I happen to be on it." Jessica smiled sweetly.

Aaron shook his head. "You're pretty amazing, Jessica."

Jessica glowed with satisfaction. Aaron was actually complimenting her in front of all these people!

Bruce pushed back his chair and stood up. "We should get going, guys."

Aaron and Jake stood up, too. "See you, Jessica," Aaron told her. He turned to leave, then turned back again. "Hey, I've got a great idea!" he exclaimed. "My parents are taking me to see a Lakers game a week from Sunday. I know we've got an extra ticket. Would you like to come along?"

Jessica waited for either Jake or Bruce to answer, but they remained silent. Everybody seemed to be looking at her expectantly.

"Well?" Aaron prompted.

Aaron was talking to *her*? Jessica's eyes widened in excitement. *Aaron Dallas had just asked her out on a date*!

"I mean, if you don't want to, that's OK," Aaron mumbled, sensing Jessica's confusion.

"No!" Jessica cried. "I mean, *yes*! I'd love to go, Aaron!"

"OK, then," Aaron said. "I'll talk to you later."

As the three boys walked away, the Unicorns sat in stunned silence.

Belinda Layton, who was on the girls' basketball team with Jessica, was the first to speak. "Jessica, you are so lucky!"

"She sure is," Mary Wallace agreed. "Aaron Dallas is awfully cute."

"I meant because she gets to go to a Lakers game," Belinda said. "Although Aaron is adorable, too."

Jessica watched Aaron, Jake, and Bruce drop off their lunch trays and head out the cafeteria door. Aaron turned around before leaving and waved to Jessica.

"I can't believe it." Jessica sighed.

"Me neither," Lila muttered.

"Me neither." Ellen frowned.

"An actual date," Jessica murmured with satisfaction.

"Don't get too carried away, Jess. It's not like you're the first person in the history of the world to go out on a date," Lila said in a sour voice.

"I'll bet I'm the first sixth grader at Sweet Valley Middle School to have a date," Jessica replied.

"How about that time we were all at the bowling alley?" Ellen retorted.

"That was just a bunch of guys and girls meeting somewhere," Mary pointed out. "It wasn't really a date, Ellen."

"Well, anyway, I don't see why Aaron asked *Jessica*," Lila grumbled. "He could have asked any of us."

"Maybe it's because he knows she likes basketball," Belinda suggested. "You aren't exactly a big fan, Lila."

As her friends continued to argue, Jessica sat back in her chair and basked in her moment of glory. She knew the *real* reason Aaron had asked her out. It was obviously because she, Jessica Wakefield, was the prettiest and most popular girl in the whole sixth grade!

Jessica pushed back her chair and stood up.

"Where are you going?" Ellen asked.

Jessica nodded toward the food line. "To get a piece of chocolate cake. Suddenly I'm starving!"

Two

◇

"There you are!" Mr. Bowman looked up from his desk and smiled broadly. "Come on in and have a seat, Elizabeth."

Elizabeth slid into a front-row seat in the empty classroom. "You wanted to see me?" she asked.

Mr. Bowman reached for a newspaper on his desk and walked over to Elizabeth. As usual, he was wearing clothes that didn't match—green slacks, a bright orange shirt, and a red-and-pink striped tie. But Elizabeth didn't care how Mr. Bowman dressed. He was her favorite teacher because he made learning so much fun.

"I need your help, Elizabeth," Mr. Bowman began.

"Sure," Elizabeth replied. "What's the problem?"

Mr. Bowman perched on the desk next to Elizabeth. "I got a call today from the *Sweet Valley Tribune*. They've begun a new feature in the paper called the 'Junior Journalist' column. Each week, a student from a local school writes an article for the paper."

"That sounds pretty exciting," Elizabeth said.

"Besides the chance to work for a real daily newspaper, the Junior Journalists get paid fifty dollars each for their stories." Mr. Bowman rubbed his chin. "So here's my problem. The *Tribune* asked me to pick a promising student to represent Sweet Valley Middle School as a Junior Journalist. He or she should have newspaper experience—the kind the editor of a school newspaper might have. And he or she should really love writing." He scratched the back of his head. "Sound like anyone you know?"

Elizabeth couldn't help but smile. "It sounds a lot like me."

"That's exactly what I thought." Mr. Bowman shook Elizabeth's hand. "Congratulations, Junior Journalist. I think you'll do a fine job representing Sweet Valley Middle School."

Elizabeth could hardly believe her ears. She was

going to have an article printed in a real newspaper! "But what should I write about?" she asked.

"The editors have already chosen a topic. They want an article about 'Students Who Make a Difference.' It should be about students who benefit the community or their school in some significant way."

"That shouldn't be too hard." Elizabeth thought for a moment. "There are a lot of students at Sweet Valley Middle School who do volunteer work and perform community service."

"Well, the article is due in two weeks, so you have plenty of time to decide who you want to write about," Mr. Bowman said. "But whomever you decide on, I'm sure you'll do a great job, Elizabeth."

"Thanks, Mr. Bowman!" Elizabeth said excitedly as she leapt out of her chair. "I won't let you down, I promise."

"Where are you off to in such a hurry?" Mr. Bowman laughed at Elizabeth's enthusiasm.

"I'm going to start to work on my article right away!"

"Here." Mr. Bowman handed her his newspaper. "Take this copy of the *Tribune* with you. There's an article by a Junior Journalist from Weston Middle School in here. It might give you some ideas."

Elizabeth took the newspaper and raced out the door. She couldn't wait to tell Jessica her big news. She remembered that Jessica was at a Boosters practice. So she dashed toward the gym.

The Boosters were just finishing a baton routine as Elizabeth came running into the gym.

"That was *much* better," Janet Howell told the group. Janet, an eighth grader, was president of the Unicorns and head of the Boosters. "If we keep up the good work, we'll be the hit of the next pep rally!"

The Boosters applauded themselves, with the exception of Amy Sutton. Amy, Elizabeth's closest friend next to her twin, was the only girl on the Boosters squad who wasn't a Unicorn or a close friend of a Unicorn. Like Elizabeth, she thought the Unicorns were boring snobs, but she had joined the Boosters because she was an excellent baton twirler.

After Janet dismissed the girls from practice, Amy ran over to join her friend.

"I've got exciting news!" Elizabeth told Amy.

"So does your sister." Amy nodded toward Jessica, who was coming over to join them.

"What is it?" Elizabeth wanted to know.

"You'll know soon⁻enough, believe me. We've been hearing about it all through practice," Amy said.

"Lizzie!" Jessica cried. "I've got the most amazing news!"

"Me, too!" Elizabeth replied. "You go first."

"Guess who is going to be the very first sixth grader at Sweet Valley Middle School to go on a *real* date?" Jessica asked importantly.

"Guess who's going to drive us all insane talking about her stupid date?" Lila snapped as she joined them.

"She's just jealous," Jessica explained breezily.

"A date?" Elizabeth asked. "Where? With whom?"

"To a Lakers game with Aaron Dallas," Lila answered for Jessica. "I can't believe you haven't heard by now. I'm sure it'll be on the evening news."

"Jess! That's great!" Elizabeth was truly happy for her sister.

"He asked me during lunchtime at the Unicorner," Jessica said dreamily.

"How romantic." Amy rolled her eyes.

"It *was* romantic." Jessica turned to Elizabeth. "Amy's just jealous, too."

"Oh, please." Amy laughed sharply. "I mean, Aaron's very nice and everything, but I wouldn't want to go on a date with him."

"When are you going?" Elizabeth asked.

"A week from Sunday," Jessica answered.

"Which is good, because I'll have plenty of time to decide what to wear. And, of course, to plan the conversation."

"Plan the conversation?" Lila echoed. "What do you mean, 'plan the conversation'?"

"Lila, don't you know anything? I read an article in *Smash!* called 'How to Rate as a Great First Date,' " Jessica explained. "The article said you should plan your conversation in advance so you always have lots to talk about."

"Give me a break!" Amy groaned.

"Speaking of articles," Elizabeth said, "I have some news of my own."

"Tell us!" Amy thought it was time to change the subject.

"Well, I just met with Mr. Bowman. The *Sweet Valley Tribune* is inviting students to be Junior Journalists. Each Junior Journalist writes an article about his or her school, and it gets published in the *Tribune*. Anyway, Mr. Bowman asked *me* to represent Sweet Valley Middle School!"

"Congratulations, Elizabeth!" Jessica exclaimed, patting her twin on the back.

"Elizabeth! That's fantastic!" Amy's enthusiasm was genuine, but she couldn't help looking a little disappointed.

"Oh, Amy, Mr. Bowman only asked me because I'm the editor of the *Sixers*," Elizabeth explained quickly. Amy also worked hard on the sixth-grade newspaper, and Elizabeth hated to think her friend felt left out. "And I could really use some help doing the research for the article."

Amy brightened. "Great! What's the topic?"

" 'Students Who Make a Difference.' " Elizabeth opened the newspaper Mr. Bowman had given her so they could see the Junior Journalist's article.

"Wow!" Amy breathed. "Imagine, Elizabeth! Your name in print in a real newspaper! Your first professional byline."

Jessica leaned toward Elizabeth, her brow wrinkled. "What does that headline say, anyway?" she asked impatiently.

" 'Weston Students Brighten the Lives of Nursing Home Residents,' " Elizabeth read.

"Big deal," Lila said. "I'm sure you're going to write about much more important things. Right, Elizabeth?"

"Like what, Lila?" Amy asked.

"I don't know. *Interesting* people," Lila said vaguely.

"Like the Unicorns!" Jessica blurted. "Why not do a profile of us, Elizabeth? We're the most interesting people in school. Especially now," she added proudly. "Maybe you could cover my date with Aaron."

Elizabeth tried not to smile. "The article is supposed to be about students who do good deeds," she reminded her sister.

"And when have the Unicorns ever done anything to help anybody?" Amy asked, crossing her arms over her chest.

Lila and Jessica looked at each other.

"Well?" Amy prompted.

"Give us a minute!" Lila snapped.

Amy tapped her sneaker on the shiny gym floor. "We're waiting."

"I know!" Jessica cried. "Yesterday, when we were in the girls' bathroom!" She nudged Lila in the ribs with her elbow. "Remember, Lila?"

Lila nodded firmly. "That's right."

"Janet was touching up her mascara," Jessica explained, "and she decided she didn't really like the color anymore. But instead of throwing the mascara away, she left it by the sink in case someone else would want it. Someone less fortunate."

Elizabeth looked at Amy, and both girls burst out laughing.

"That's very noble, Jessica," Amy said at last. "But I don't think it's exactly what the *Tribune* has in mind. Come on, Elizabeth. Let's start the work on your article."

"Be sure to save some space for the Unicorns!" Lila called as Elizabeth and Amy walked away.

"You'll have to do better than the Mascara Charity," Elizabeth answered over her shoulder.

"We will!" Lila cried. "Just wait and see!"

Elizabeth looked at Amy and winked. "That'll be the day!"

That night at dinner, Jessica let Elizabeth talk about her article for the *Tribune*. Elizabeth's news wasn't nearly as exciting as her own, but Jessica wanted to wait until just the right moment to make her grand announcement.

When the family began to eat their dessert, Jessica found her moment.

"Mom, Dad, I have something very important to tell you," she said seriously.

"Is something wrong, honey?" Mrs. Wakefield asked.

"No, Mom, something's *right*! I'm going on my first date!"

Steven, who had just taken a drink of milk, snorted, spraying milk all over his plate.

"Gross, Steven!" Jessica cried.

"I'll tell you what's gross," Steven exclaimed as he wiped up the milk with his napkin. "The idea of *you* going on a date!"

Jessica tipped up her chin defiantly, turned her attention to her parents, and waited for their excited response.

"What do you mean by 'date'?" Mr. Wakefield asked, looking concerned. "Do you mean with a boy?"

"Of course with a boy, Dad," Jessica said patiently. "Aaron Dallas asked me to go to the Lakers game a week from Sunday."

"Are his parents going?" Mrs. Wakefield asked.

Jessica nodded. Her parents weren't nearly as excited as she'd hoped they would be. Didn't they understand how important this date was to her?

Mrs. Wakefield looked relieved. "Well, I suppose it's all right then. What do you think, Ned?"

"As long as it's just a basketball game and Aaron's parents are there to supervise, I think it'll be fine." He winked at Mrs. Wakefield. "And I'd hate to have Jessica miss a chance to see the Lakers play!"

"This is so unfair," Steven moaned. "Why should Aaron waste a perfectly good ticket on you? Wouldn't he rather take someone who can appreciate the game? Me, for example."

"Your sister's a terrific basketball player, Steven," Mr. Wakefield reminded him. "I'm sure she'll enjoy the game."

"Well, I still say it isn't fair," Steven grumbled.

After they had finished clearing up the dishes, Jessica and Elizabeth went upstairs to do their homework. Before she set to work, Elizabeth opened the copy of the *Tribune* Mr. Bowman had given her and began to read it through carefully. But she hadn't even gotten halfway through an article when Jessica entered her room, rubbing her forehead.

"What's wrong, Jess?" Elizabeth asked, setting aside the paper.

Jessica sat down on the edge of Elizabeth's bed. "I've got such a headache. I've been reading that story Mr. Bowman assigned us, and I guess I've just been working too long."

"But we only came upstairs twenty minutes ago."

Jessica fell back onto the bed dramatically and rubbed her eyes. "I'll *never* be able to finish the assignment now! Couldn't you just tell me how the story ends, Lizzie?"

"They all live happily ever after."

Jessica smiled with relief. "That's what I figured."

Elizabeth shook her head. "Don't you think you should read the entire story? What if Mr. Bowman gives us a quiz?"

"He won't," Jessica said confidently. "He just gave us one two days ago."

"Still—"

"And besides," Jessica interrupted, "there's no way I could concentrate on homework tonight!

Every time I try to pay attention to what's on the page, I picture Aaron at the Unicorner today." Jessica sighed. "He has the most beautiful brown eyes, Elizabeth."

"You really like him a lot, don't you?"

Jessica nodded dreamily. "A *lot*." Suddenly, she sat up on her elbows. "That reminds me. I've got work to do!"

"You mean homework?"

"No." Jessica laughed and leapt off the bed. "*Clothes* work! I've got to decide what to wear tomorrow. It's important that I look my absolute best."

"To impress Aaron?" Elizabeth asked.

"To impress *everyone*," Jessica explained, as if it were the most obvious thing in the world. "Everybody will be watching me tomorrow."

"Why?" Elizabeth was puzzled.

Jessica tossed her hair back over her shoulder. "Because your sister is the talk of Sweet Valley Middle School! By tomorrow, everyone will know about my date with Aaron."

"Don't you think you're getting just a little carried away, Jess? I know you're excited about your date, but going to a basketball game with a boy and his family isn't exactly front-page news."

Jessica put her hands on her hips. "Didn't you

notice Lila and Amy after Boosters practice? They were green with envy!"

"Maybe Lila was jealous, but I don't think Amy cared one way or the other," Elizabeth replied. "I just don't want you to get too carried away."

Jessica threw her hands up in the air. "There's no point in discussing this with you, Elizabeth. You simply don't understand the responsibilities of being popular!" Jessica whirled around and stomped out of the room.

Too bad her date isn't sooner, Elizabeth said to herself. *I may not be able to stand much more of this!*

Three

◇

"Jessica Wakefield, if you don't let me in right this minute, I'm breaking this door down!" Elizabeth threatened on Thursday morning. "We're going to be late for school!"

Jessica opened the bathroom door a few inches. "There's no need to yell, Elizabeth," she said calmly. "So what if we're a few minutes late? I have to look my best today."

Elizabeth glared at her twin. "You're going to look your *worst* when I get through with you, unless you let me into this bathroom by the time I count to three! One . . . two . . ."

"All right, all right!" Jessica pulled the door open all the way.

Elizabeth stepped into the bathroom and gasped. There were clothes strewn everywhere, and the counter was littered with Jessica's makeup and jewelry.

"I'll clean it up later," Jessica said breezily as she applied a light coat of gloss to her lips.

"Is that Mom's expensive perfume I smell?" Elizabeth stepped closer to Jessica and sniffed the air.

"Boys like a girl to smell nice," Jessica informed her sister.

"Maybe so, but I'll bet Mom's not going to like your using her perfume."

"I only used a few drops!" Jessica protested as she continued to admire her image in the mirror.

"Then why do you smell like a perfume factory?"

"How do I look, anyway?" Jessica asked, ignoring Elizabeth's remark.

"Fine. But I don't see why it took you an entire hour to get ready."

"Do you like my outfit?" Jessica pressed.

Elizabeth nodded as she put toothpaste on her brush.

"You don't seem very enthusiastic."

"Jessica, I've seen your purple skirt about a zillion times," Elizabeth pointed out. "You already know I like it."

"Do you think Aaron will like it?" Jessica asked.

"How should I know?" Elizabeth glanced at her watch. "I've got five minutes to brush my teeth, comb my hair, and walk to school, Jess. Could we discuss Aaron some other time?"

"Five minutes!" Jessica gasped. "Hurry up, Elizabeth! You're going to make me late for school!"

One look at her twin's expression told Jessica she would be safer in the hallway. She dashed out of the bathroom just as Steven was starting down the stairs.

Steven sniffed the air curiously. "What stinks?"

"It's a very sophisticated perfume called 'Memorable,' " Jessica replied coolly.

"What did you do, use the whole bottle?" Steven clamped his nose shut with two fingers. "You're definitely memorable, shrimp!" Then he put his hands around his neck and pretended to stagger down the stairs. "Help! I can't breathe!"

Jessica started to respond, but then reconsidered. She spun around and headed to the bathroom to wash off some of the perfume. As much as she hated to admit it, Steven might have a point. If he didn't like the way she smelled, Aaron might not either. After all, Steven was a boy—even if he was her brother.

That morning at school, it seemed as if all Jessica could think about was Aaron. *Of course*, she told herself, *it's only natural*. Everywhere she went, she could tell people were talking about her date. When she walked down the hall, kids she didn't even know seemed to nod and smile at her. She felt like a celebrity.

Jessica spent most of math class writing the initials *A.D.* all over her notebook. When she heard Ms. Wyler call her name near the end of class, she looked up in surprise from her daydream.

"Yes?" she asked, quickly covering her notebook with her hand.

Ms. Wyler impatiently tapped a piece of chalk on the blackboard. "The answer to this equation, please."

Fortunately, it was an easy problem. Jessica took just a moment to figure it out in her head. "Five hundred and fifty-seven," she answered confidently.

Some of the other students snickered.

"Did you say five hundred and fifty-seven?" Ms. Wyler peered at her through her glasses.

Jessica glanced over her shoulder at Lila and Ellen. She could tell from their smiles that they knew something she didn't.

"Um, yes," Jessica replied quietly. "Five hundred and fifty-seven."

Someone else giggled. Jessica stared at the

board. *What is going on here?* she wondered. *The answer is so obvious!*

"Would you mind telling us how you arrived at that number?" Ms. Wyler inquired patiently.

Jessica squirmed in her chair. "I just added the two numbers together."

"Why would you add the numbers, when there's a minus sign in the equation?"

"A minus sign?" Jessica squinted at the board. Sure enough, she had misread the equation.

"Ms. Wyler?" Lila called, waving her hand. "I know the answer! It's four hundred and ninety-two."

Jessica glanced back at Lila, who gave her a superior smile.

She's just trying to get back at me because she's jealous about Aaron, Jessica consoled herself. Still, it was embarrassing to have missed such an easy question. If she hadn't misread the problem, she would have known the answer for sure.

Jessica shrugged and returned to her doodling. By the time class was over, she had forgotten all about her mistake. As the class filed out the door, she caught up with Lila and Ellen.

"I can't wait until lunch," she told them. "Do you think Aaron will stop by the Unicorner again?"

Lila shrugged. "I hope not. I don't think I could stand to hear another basketball conversation!"

"You can say that again!" Ellen paused, sniffed the air, and gave Jessica a quizzical look. "Are you wearing perfume?"

Jessica nodded. "It's called 'Memorable.' Don't you love it?"

"Did you use the whole bottle?" Lila snickered.

Jessica sniffed her wrist. "I thought I washed most of it off. Besides," she added defensively, "I'm sure Aaron will like it."

"I doubt it," Lila predicted.

"Who's the one going on the date with him?" Jessica demanded. "You or me?"

Lila sighed heavily. "Aaron, Aaron, Aaron! Is he all you can talk about?"

"Yeah. Why don't you find somebody else to bore?" Ellen chimed in.

"Fine!" Jessica shot back. "I didn't realize you two were so jealous!"

Jessica leaned against a locker and watched Lila and Ellen walk off. *I'm just going to have to get used to this,* she told herself. *People are always jealous of the most popular students.*

"Uh, hello, Jessica."

Jessica looked up to see Mandy Miller standing in front of her. Mandy was a girl who had been hanging around the Unicorns lately. The Unicorns had often laughed about her thrift-store wardrobe and about how she tagged along behind the Unicorns like a puppy. Mandy seemed particularly fond of Jessica, a fact that usually drove Jessica crazy.

But today Jessica didn't mind her at all. "Hi, Mandy. I don't suppose you happened to hear about Aaron and me, did you?"

"Oh, *everybody* knows about you two." Mandy smiled. "You're the hottest couple since Romeo and Juliet."

"Thanks." For a moment, Jessica wasn't quite sure if Mandy was joking. "Would you like to hear about how he asked me out?"

"Sure," Mandy said eagerly.

"Great! It's so nice to find someone who isn't consumed with jealousy. It all started at the Unicorner," Jessica began, as the two girls headed down the hallway.

"We have something very important to discuss today," Janet announced at lunch.

"You mean my date?" Jessica tore open a package of corn chips.

"I know it's hard to believe, Jessica, but that's *not* what I had in mind," Janet replied.

"We have more important things to discuss," Lila added.

Jessica rolled her eyes. It was obvious that each and every one of the Unicorns was jealous. She glanced around the lunchroom, hoping to catch sight of Aaron, but he was nowhere to be seen.

"By now, everybody's heard about Elizabeth's newspaper project, right?" Janet asked.

"What does that have to do with us?" Jessica demanded.

"Elizabeth's article is going to be in the *Sweet Valley Tribune*," Janet replied. "Maybe even on the front page. It's our big chance to have the whole town know about the Unicorns! There might even be pictures!"

"But Elizabeth said the article had to be about good deeds," Jessica pointed out. "You know— like the work I did helping clean up the beach after the oil spill. That sort of thing."

"That doesn't mean we couldn't do something charitable just this once, to be sure we're the focus of Elizabeth's article," Lila argued.

"And this is a good chance to make up for that time we tried to publish our own paper," Janet added.

There was silence at the table. No one liked to remember *that* humiliating experience. When the *Sixers* hadn't printed a story Jessica had written about the Unicorns, the Unicorns had tried to launch their own paper, featuring only Unicorn news. Unfortunately, the project had been short-lived.

"I guess you're right, Janet," Jessica said at last. "If we were in the *Tribune*, everyone would know about the Unicorns. The publicity would be a thousand times better than what we could have gotten by printing our own paper."

"But what could we do that Elizabeth would want to write about?" Ellen asked as she opened her carton of milk.

"Well, the theme of the article is 'Students Who Make a Difference,' " Janet reminded them.

"A difference doing what?" Kimberly asked.

"You know," Jessica said, "noble stuff."

"Good deeds," Lila added, unwrapping her tuna fish sandwich.

"We'll have to come up with something really big," Janet said seriously. "We'll be competing with lots of other kids who have more experience than we have doing good. We should brainstorm right now."

"I'll make a list." Belinda reached for her notebook and a pencil. "OK. I'm ready!"

For several minutes no one said a word.

"Maybe we should raise money for something," Jessica suggested at last.

"Great idea!" Janet said approvingly. "What?"

Jessica shrugged. "I don't know."

"It should be something everyone at school can use," Mary pointed out. "Not just the Unicorns."

"Good point, Mary," Janet agreed.

"I know!" Lila exclaimed. "New uniforms for the Boosters!"

Janet shook her head. "We just said the money is supposed to be for everybody, Lila."

Lila frowned. "Well, everybody at school looks at us when we do our routines. Don't you think they'd like to see us in new outfits?"

Janet considered the idea. "Write it down, Belinda."

"How about a TV in the lunchroom so we can keep up with our soap operas?" Ellen suggested.

"Much better!" Janet pronounced. "Everybody would enjoy that."

"TVs are awfully expensive, though," Jessica pointed out. "And Elizabeth's article is due in two weeks. We don't have time to raise a lot of money."

"Besides, who would decide what channel to watch?" Janet added wisely. She turned to Belinda. "Don't bother writing that one down. The principal probably wouldn't let us have a TV anyway."

For a few minutes the group was silent. "I've got it!" Kimberly cried at last. "What's something we're always saying we need in the girls' locker room?"

"Deodorant?" Lila ventured.

Kimberly rolled her eyes. "No—*curling irons!*"

"That's brilliant!" Janet exclaimed. "We'll buy a couple of curling irons and leave them in the locker room for everyone to use after gym class. It's the perfect way for us to make a difference without having to do any work!"

"Or spend much money," Ellen added.

"Of course, there's one problem," Belinda said quietly. "What about the boys? I mean, shouldn't we be doing something that benefits both the boys and the girls?"

Janet slumped in her chair. "I suppose you have a point, Belinda." She sighed. "This doing-good stuff isn't very easy."

"If we want to be featured in the article, we need to come up with something Elizabeth would consider noble," Jessica told her friends. "And Elizabeth doesn't even *use* a curling iron."

"All right. Do you have any ideas?" Ellen asked.

Jessica thought long and hard. "How about something for the library?" she suggested. "We could buy some books or something. Or maybe a new encyclopedia set. That old set smells like mildew."

"The librarian told me it's because the roof leaked last year," Belinda said.

"Jessica, I think you're onto something," Janet said approvingly. "How can Elizabeth pass up a chance to write about the Unicorns when we tell

her we're going to buy the school a new encyclopedia set? It's perfect!"

"But how will we pay for it?" Mary asked.

"We'll decide that later," Janet replied. "I think
we should have a special meeting on Saturday.
After all, we don't have much time to plan. But
we can't meet at my house. My parents are having
the living room painted this weekend."

"We can meet at my house." Jessica loved to
have the Unicorns over.

Just then, Aaron walked by the Unicorner carrying his lunch tray. "Hi, Jessica," he said, smiling
as he passed them.

"Hi, Aaron," Jessica replied in a syrupy-sweet
voice.

"Excuse me while I gag!" Lila pretended to
choke.

"Hi, Aaron!" Ellen mimicked in a high-pitched
voice.

But Jessica didn't even hear them. She was too
busy smiling after Aaron.

Thursday afternoon, just as Elizabeth had predicted, Mr. Bowman gave a pop quiz on the story
Jessica hadn't bothered to finish the night before.
So when he asked her to stay after class for a talk,
she wasn't entirely surprised.

Jessica waited by his desk, and watched as the

other students filed out of class. When Aaron walked by, Jessica was sure he was about to smile at her again, but someone got in the way.

"I'm really sorry about the quiz," Jessica blurted out as soon as everyone was gone and she was alone with Mr. Bowman. "I had a terrible headache last night, and I just couldn't finish the story. But I promise I'll get an A on the next quiz."

Mr. Bowman laughed. "Slow down a minute! I didn't ask you to stay after class so we could talk about your quiz. Although I *do* hope you'll try to catch up on your reading tonight."

"You didn't?" Jessica sighed with relief.

Mr. Bowman shook his head. "Have you been having a lot of headaches lately, Jessica?"

"Some," she answered. "Mostly when I read at night."

"I've noticed you squinting at the board a lot, too."

"Squinting? Me?" Jessica shifted nervously. She didn't like the sound of Mr. Bowman's voice. Mr. Bowman loved to joke around, but all of a sudden, he seemed very serious.

"I think you should have your eyes examined, Jessica," he said gently.

"Examined?" She repeated uneasily.

"Yes, Jessica. To see if you need glasses."

Four

◇

"Glasses!" Jessica shrieked.

As soon as the word was out of her mouth, she spun around to make certain no one had heard her. She didn't want to start any crazy rumors!

"We won't know anything for sure until you have your eyes tested," Mr. Bowman said in a reassuring voice. "But if it does turn out that you need glasses, Jessica, it won't be the end of the world." He smiled kindly. "Some of the most fashionable people I know wear glasses!"

Jessica looked at Mr. Bowman's polka-dot bow tie and plaid shirt. What could he possibly know about fashion?

"Glasses are for nerds like Randy Mason and

Lois Waller!" she declared emphatically. "Unicorns don't wear glasses!"

Jessica could tell from Mr. Bowman's frown that he disapproved of what she had said. But it was true. She was just not the kind of person who wore glasses. She was popular. She was pretty. She had a date with Aaron Dallas.

But she knew better than to argue with a teacher, especially a teacher who had just given a pop quiz she had probably flunked.

Jessica gave Mr. Bowman one of her very best smiles. "Really, Mr. Bowman," she began sweetly, "I can see just *fine*. But I appreciate your concern."

That should do it, she thought with satisfaction. *Teachers like to feel helpful.*

Mr. Bowman fiddled with his bow tie. "Just to be on the safe side, though, I think you should have your eyes checked by an eye doctor."

Jessica looked down at her feet. "All right," she said. "I'll be sure to mention it to my parents." *A few years from now*, she added silently.

"Good. And just in case they have any questions, I've written this note for you to give them." Mr. Bowman reached into his shirt pocket and handed Jessica an envelope.

Thanks a million, Jessica thought in frustration. Reluctantly, she took the envelope.

"Be sure to give this to your parents," Mr. Bowman said.

"I will," Jessica muttered. "But you don't understand, Mr. Bowman. I really don't need glasses. Glasses are for people who study all the time."

"Are you sure you don't want to rephrase that?" he asked, grinning.

Jessica felt her cheeks begin to redden. "I meant that only geeks wear glasses."

Mr. Bowman reached into his other shirt pocket and pulled out a pair of black horn-rimmed glasses. He perched them on his nose and smiled. "I wouldn't jump to conclusions, Jessica," he chided. "As it happens, I wear glasses when I'm reading. And I'm certainly not a geek!"

Jessica took one look at Mr. Bowman standing there in his thick black glasses and polka-dot tie, and she had all the proof she needed.

She wouldn't be caught dead wearing glasses!

As she and Elizabeth walked home from school, Jessica thought about what Mr. Bowman had said. The more she thought about it, the angrier she got. He had some nerve, suggesting that she, of all people, couldn't see very well! Jessica closed one eye, opened it, then closed the other. Houses, cars, sidewalk, stop sign—she could see them without any trouble at all.

"Elizabeth," Jessica asked casually as they turned the corner onto their tree-lined street, "can you read the license plate on that blue car parked across the street from our house?"

Elizabeth squinted. "No. It's a few blocks away. Why?"

"Just curious." Jessica smiled with relief. Elizabeth's eyes were no better than Jessica's. And if Elizabeth didn't need glasses, neither did Jessica. After all, they *were* identical twins.

"Is everything OK, Jess?" Elizabeth asked as they walked up the Wakefields' driveway. "You've been awfully quiet all the way home."

"What could be wrong?" Jessica responded lightly. She glanced down at her backpack and noticed that Mr. Bowman's letter was sticking out just a bit. Quickly, she pushed it inside before they reached the kitchen.

While Elizabeth stopped to chat with their mother, Jessica headed straight upstairs to her room. She pulled the envelope out of her backpack and held it up to the light. For a moment she considered opening it, but then she realized she didn't have to. She already knew what it said: *Dear Mr. and Mrs. Wakefield, Your daughter is as blind as a bat.*

The real question was how to get rid of the letter. If she threw it away, somebody might spot it in the trash. It would be safer to hide it in her room, at least for now. Jessica herself had a tough time finding anything in her room. It was always a disaster area.

Suddenly, she had a brilliant idea. Her mattress! Nobody would ever look under there. Jessica tossed aside a pile of clothes and lifted up a corner of her mattress. For a split second, she felt a pang of guilt about hiding Mr. Bowman's letter. But there was no point in needlessly upsetting her parents. She would be doing them a favor by hiding the stupid note.

Jessica pushed the envelope as far underneath her mattress as she could reach.

"Jess?" Elizabeth asked, pushing her sister's door open a few inches.

"What?" Jessica snapped, dropping the mattress and whirling around. "Do you have to sneak up on me like that, Elizabeth?"

Elizabeth stepped inside the room. "I knocked, but I guess you didn't hear me."

"I suppose you think I'm deaf, on top of everything else!" Jessica said testily.

"What are you talking about?"

"Never mind." Jessica plopped down on the edge of her bed.

Elizabeth narrowed her eyes. "What were you hiding under there, anyway?"

"Hiding?"

"Don't try to fool me, Jessica." Elizabeth put her hands on her hips. "I know you too well."

Jessica picked a shirt off the floor and occupied herself with folding it. Sometimes it was better to ignore Elizabeth when she started asking questions.

"Jessica, you might as well tell me. You know you will, eventually."

"It's not important," Jessica replied.

"Sure. That explains why you hid it under your mattress." Elizabeth sat down next to Jessica on the bed. "I know something's bothering you," she said. "Maybe I can help. Come on, Jess."

Jessica forced herself to laugh. "Mr. Bowman actually thinks *I* might need glasses! Isn't that incredible?"

"Glasses!" Elizabeth exclaimed. "Why would he think that?"

"Just because I squint sometimes, and I've been getting headaches lately. And I have trouble reading the board. But so do lots of people." She turned to Elizabeth. "Honestly, Elizabeth, I see perfectly."

"Is that what that letter was about?"

Jessica nodded miserably. "Mr. Bowman told me to give it to Mom and Dad."

Elizabeth thought for a moment. "It wouldn't

be such a bad idea to have your eyes checked, Jess. Just to be on the safe side." She gave Jessica a reassuring smile. "Even though you know Mr. Bowman's wrong."

Jessica stood up abruptly. "I do *not* need glasses, Elizabeth. And even if I did, I would never wear them. I'd be the laughingstock of the whole school. The Unicorns would take away my membership. I'd have to hang around with Lois Waller and Randy Mason. It would mean permanent nerdhood!"

Elizabeth tried to look serious, but Jessica could see that she wanted to smile.

"I'm glad you're so amused!" Jessica snapped. "Maybe you should have *your* eyes checked, too. After all, we *are* twins. If I need glasses, you probably do, too."

"I wouldn't mind," Elizabeth replied calmly. "Actually, I've seen some frames that are really cute. I love Sara Hayward's glasses."

"Drop it, will you?" Jessica pleaded.

"All right. But I really think you should at least give Mr. Bowman's letter to Mom and Dad."

"I'll think about it," Jessica said curtly. "Just promise me you'll keep quiet for now."

Elizabeth sighed. "If that's what you want."

"Good." Jessica felt relieved. "So what did you want, anyway?"

"Oh, I almost forgot. I wanted to see if you felt like going for a bike ride. Steven adjusted the handlebars on my bike, and I wanted to try them out. We've got plenty of time before dinner."

"Sure," Jessica agreed. "I just need to change my clothes."

Fifteen minutes later, the twins were on their bikes. It was a beautiful afternoon, and Jessica began to feel better. It was hard to stay mad at Mr. Bowman on a day like today, particularly when she had so much to be excited about. Like Aaron.

"Where should we ride?" Elizabeth asked as they pedaled down their street.

"I have an idea," Jessica said casually. "Why don't we ride down toward Myrtle Avenue?"

"Myrtle? What's over there?"

"You mean *who's* over there." Jessica grinned mischievously. "I just might have browsed through the phone book last night."

"Through the 'D' section?" Elizabeth suggested. "D as in Dallas?"

"I was just wondering where Aaron lives," Jessica said innocently as they pulled to a stop at an intersection. "Couldn't we just sort of happen to ride by, Elizabeth? It's only a few blocks away."

"But what if you see him?"

"That's the whole *point!*" Jessica rolled her eyes. Sometimes her twin could be very dense.

The girls turned the corner. As they rode down the wide, sunny avenue, Elizabeth talked about her Junior Journalist project.

"So far I've narrowed it down to three groups."

"Only three?" Jessica teased. "I thought Sweet Valley Middle School had hundreds of do-gooders to choose from!"

Elizabeth smiled. "There's the Glee Club. It's organizing sing-alongs for people at the old-age home. And the Chess Club, which is playing chess by mail with kids in foreign countries. And Amy suggested the two kids who are studying for the National Spelling Bee."

Jessica listened with relief. No one was involved with anything as noble as the Unicorns' encyclopedia project. "Don't count the Unicorns out yet, Elizabeth," she warned. "We may surprise you."

"The Unicorns?" Elizabeth laughed. "The most meaningful thing you've ever done was vote for your favorite soap opera star."

Jessica wrinkled her forehead. "Who won, anyway? I can't remember."

"You're asking *me*?"

"Never mind. I remember now! It was Jake Sommers from *Days of Turmoil*," Jessica said excitedly.

Elizabeth groaned.

"He's an excellent actor, Elizabeth," Jessica informed her. "He also happens to be incredibly cute."

"As cute as Aaron?" Elizabeth teased.

Jessica's cheeks colored. "Well, *almost*."

They reached the top of a hill and paused. "Here it is," Elizabeth announced. "Myrtle Street."

"Aaron lives at 518 Myrtle."

Elizabeth raised her eyebrow. "You memorized his address?"

Jessica threw her sister a warning glance. She squinted at the number on the house across the street. "That means he probably lives near the far end of the street, almost at the bottom of the hill."

"So what do we do now?" Elizabeth giggled. "I feel like a spy!"

"Just act natural," Jessica instructed. "We'll ride down the hill until we find his house. Then we'll ride past it again—if we have the nerve."

"That'll look *really* natural!" Elizabeth commented dryly.

Jessica began to glide down the hill, squinting at house numbers as she rode. Her bike began to pick up speed, and she left Elizabeth far behind. "506, 508, 510," she counted off the numbers. Jessica could barely make out the house numbers until she was very close to them.

Out of the corner of her eye, Jessica saw a large piece of white paper blow out into the street. She ignored it and focused again on the passing house numbers.

Suddenly, Jessica was distracted by a pair of bright green eyes looking up at her in terror. The piece of paper was not paper at all. It was a frightened white cat, and the front wheel of her bike was only a few feet away from it!

Jessica squeezed her brakes, and her front wheel swerved. The bike went spinning out of control and slammed into the curb.

The bike stopped there, but Jessica kept going. In a flash of panic, she realized she was flying through the air!

Five

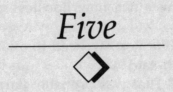

"Jessica!" Elizabeth screamed. "Are you all right?"

Jessica sat up slowly, brushing off her elbows. As far as she could tell, nothing was hurt—nothing, that is, but her pride. She glanced around for her bike. It lay in the street a few feet away from a mailbox with the number *518* painted on it.

518! She was in Aaron's yard!

Elizabeth dropped her bike by the curb and dashed over to her sister. "Are you hurt?"

"No, I'm fine," Jessica whispered, quickly getting to her feet. "Let's get out of here, Elizabeth! This is Aaron's yard!"

"Hey, Jessica! Are you OK?"

Even before she turned around, Jessica knew it

was Aaron. "Oh, no," she moaned. "How humiliating!"

Aaron jumped off the front porch and ran to Jessica's side. "What happened?" he asked breathlessly. "That was a great somersault!"

Jessica combed her fingers through her hair. "I was just trying out a new Boosters routine," she tried to joke.

"It looked like you swerved to avoid that white cat," Elizabeth said.

"White cat? That was probably Barney, my little sister's stupid cat." Aaron shook his head apologetically. "I'm really sorry, Jessica. That cat has the IQ of a rock."

"It's not your fault, Aaron," Jessica assured him. "I didn't see him until—until it was too late."

Aaron touched her lightly on the shoulder. "Still, you could have been really hurt."

Jessica couldn't answer. Her eyes were fixed on Aaron's hand on her shoulder.

"Would you like something to drink, maybe?" Aaron asked awkwardly as he took his hand away.

"Drink?" Jessica echoed, a dreamy smile plastered on her face.

"Thanks, Aaron, but we should be getting home," Elizabeth said, taking her sister's arm and leading her to her fallen bike.

"Well, I'll see you tomorrow at school, then," Aaron said.

"See you!" Jessica repeated, still smiling.

Elizabeth handed Jessica her bike while Aaron returned to his house.

"Can you climb down off cloud nine long enough to ride home?" Elizabeth teased.

"Did you see that, Elizabeth?" Jessica whispered. "Aaron touched my shoulder."

"It was very romantic," Elizabeth told her. "Can we go now?"

As they climbed onto their bikes, Elizabeth cast a worried look at her twin. "You didn't see that cat at all?"

"Actually, I thought he was a big crumpled-up piece of paper," Jessica said airily. "By the time I realized it was a cat, I didn't have much time to react." She took one last look at Aaron's house before she started to pedal. "Doesn't he have the greatest eyes?" she asked in a faraway voice.

"*He* does," Elizabeth agreed. "But I'm not so sure about yours."

Jessica almost forgot about Mr. Bowman's letter until she got to English class on Friday. Fortunately, when she walked into class with Lila and settled into her seat, Mr. Bowman was busy talking to another student.

When Aaron entered the classroom, he walked straight over to Jessica. "How are you doing?" he asked, and smiled.

Jessica noticed that his grin was just a tiny bit lopsided. She thought it was adorable.

"Great," she replied. "Thanks for coming to my rescue yesterday." Out of the corner of her eye, Jessica could see Lila pretending to gag.

"Anytime." Aaron glanced up at Mr. Bowman. "Well, I'd better go sit down. Talk to you later."

"You two lovebirds make me sick," Lila hissed.

"Wait'll you go on *your* first date." Jessica gave Lila a superior smile. "Of course, in your case, that may be a while!"

Mr. Bowman started to speak, and Lila could only make a nasty face in reply.

When the bell rang to signal the end of the period, Jessica gathered up her books and headed for the door. She was halfway there when she heard Mr. Bowman call her name.

"I'd like to talk to you for just a minute," he said.

Jessica walked over to his desk, hoping he wanted to discuss the C minus she had gotten on yesterday's pop quiz, and not the note he had asked her to give to her parents.

"Yes?" she asked quietly, glancing over her

shoulder to make sure everybody had left the classroom.

"I just wanted to see how things were going with your vision problem."

"Just fine," Jessica said lightly.

"Did your parents make an appointment with an eye doctor?" Mr. Bowman pressed.

Jessica tucked a strand of hair behind her ears. "Not yet. It was too late to do anything about it yesterday."

"I see." Mr. Bowman rubbed his chin thoughtfully. "Well, have a nice weekend, Jessica."

Jessica sighed loudly. *I'm off the hook,* she thought happily. "You, too, Mr. Bowman," she said, and raced toward the door.

"And be sure to read all of that homework assignment!" he called after her.

"I promise!"

That was a close call, Jessica told herself as she tore down the hallway to safety. She hadn't really lied. And by Monday, with any luck at all, Mr. Bowman would have forgotten all about her stupid eyesight.

"I'm so glad it's Friday!" Jessica exclaimed as she stepped into the Wakefields' kitchen that afternoon.

"You can say that again!" Elizabeth dropped her

backpack onto a kitchen chair and headed for the cupboard to search for a snack.

Jessica settled into a chair. "It's been an exciting week, hasn't it, Elizabeth?"

"It certainly has." Mrs. Wakefield came into the kitchen, a frown marring her usually bright face. "We found out about Elizabeth's article for the *Tribune*, and Jessica's date, and of course—"

She paused and looked squarely at Jessica. "We also found out about Jessica's eye problem."

Jessica gulped. "Eye problem?"

Mrs. Wakefield put her hands on her hips. "When exactly did you plan to discuss this with us, Jessica? Sometime in the next decade?"

"Elizabeth!" Jessica cried. "How could you? You promised not to tell!"

"But I didn't!" Elizabeth protested.

"I'm very disappointed in you, Jessica," Mrs. Wakefield continued. "Your eyesight is nothing to play around with. Why didn't you tell us you were having trouble seeing?"

"But I'm not!" Jessica argued. "I can see just fine, Mom."

"According to Mr. Bowman, you've been having trouble reading the blackboard. And you've been complaining of headaches." Mrs. Wakefield shook her head and patted Jessica on the back.

"Getting glasses isn't a big deal, honey. Lots of attractive people wear glasses."

"Name one!" Jessica blurted.

Mrs. Wakefield smiled. "How about your father? He wears them when he's reading."

Jessica groaned. "He's a *dad*. That doesn't count." She glared at her twin. "I'll never forgive you for this, Elizabeth Wakefield!"

"Jessica, your sister had nothing to do with my knowing about this." Mrs. Wakefield said. "Mr. Bowman called a few minutes before you got home to be sure we got the letter he gave you yesterday."

"Oh." Jessica looked over at Elizabeth with a sheepish expression. "Sorry, Lizzie. I guess I got a little carried away."

Elizabeth shrugged. "That's OK, Jess. I know you're upset."

"Where exactly is the letter, Jessica?" Mrs. Wakefield asked.

"Upstairs. In my room." Jessica smiled weakly at her mother. "Under my mattress."

A grin formed on Mrs. Wakefield's face. "You really were desperate, weren't you? Look, I'd probably be madder at you, but I know how you feel about glasses, honey. Just promise me that the next time you have a problem, you won't try to hide it from us, OK?"

Jessica nodded.

"I've already made an appointment with Dr. Cruz for Monday afternoon," Mrs. Wakefield continued. "He's your father's eye doctor."

Jessica felt her stomach churn. "Monday? But that's so soon!" she cried. "Can't it wait just a little while longer? Say, until summer?"

Mrs. Wakefield stroked Jessica's hair. "No, it can't. Besides, there's no point in jumping the gun. You may not even need glasses. If you do, there are some lovely styles available that would look wonderful on you."

"That's what I told her," Elizabeth said.

Jessica looked from her mother to Elizabeth and back again. She tried to picture them wearing glasses. In her mind's eye, they looked ridiculous.

Two days from now, *she* might look ridiculous, too.

Hot tears welled up in Jessica's eyes and spilled down her cheeks. "You just don't understand!" Jessica ran from the kitchen to her bedroom and slammed the door behind her.

"Jess?" Elizabeth tapped lightly on her sister's door.

"Go away."

"Please, can I talk to you?" Even though she thought Jessica was being a little silly about her eyesight, Elizabeth hated to see her twin so unhappy.

"I guess," Jessica answered in a muffled voice.

Elizabeth opened the door. Jessica was lying on her bed with her face buried in a pillow. Slowly, she turned her head to look at Elizabeth. Her face was red and splotchy from crying.

"Jessica," Elizabeth said gently, joining her on the bed, "don't you think you're overreacting a little?"

Jessica sniffed loudly. "That's easy for you to say. You won't have to look like the biggest nerd in the universe." She rolled over onto her back. "Elizabeth, what will Aaron think if I show up at school on Tuesday wearing glasses?"

"If he stops liking you just because you're wearing glasses, then he's not worth your time to begin with," Elizabeth said logically.

"But I—I really like Aaron, Elizabeth."

Elizabeth looked at her twin in surprise. She had assumed that Jessica liked the idea of going out on a date more than she liked Aaron himself. "You really do, don't you?"

Jessica brushed away a tear with the back of her hand and nodded.

"You know, it's possible you won't even need glasses. There's no point in jumping to conclusions."

"But the truth is, Elizabeth"—Jessica took a deep breath—"my eyes *have* been bothering me lately."

"You know, I remember learning in science class that carrots are good for your eyes. Maybe you should eat a lot of carrots before your appointment with Dr. Cruz!" Elizabeth giggled.

Jessica sat up. "That's a great idea, Elizabeth!"

"But I was only joking!"

Jessica didn't seem to care. "Remember that old movie we watched on TV a few weeks ago? A boy had terrible eyesight, but it got better when he exercised his eyes."

"Exercise?" Elizabeth was puzzled.

"Yes. He followed a pencil back and forth with his eyes for hours and hours."

"But that was an old movie, Jess. There's no guarantee that exercise would help your eyes," Elizabeth argued.

"What have I got to lose? It's worth a try, isn't it?" Jessica jumped off the bed and grabbed a pencil off her desk. Slowly, she moved it back and forth in front of her face, following it with her eyes.

"Would you do me a favor, Elizabeth?" Jessica asked as she continued the pencil exercise.

"Sure. What?"

"Go downstairs and get me some carrots. I only

have two days to correct my eyesight, and I don't want to waste a single minute."

Elizabeth stood up. "How many carrots do you want?"

"As many as you can find," Jessica said.

"I'm on my way. And Jess—"

"Hmm?"

"Just remember, in case this doesn't work—you could probably wear contacts," Elizabeth said.

Jessica set the pencil down and faced Elizabeth with grim determination. "Don't worry," she said confidently. "By Monday, my eyesight will be perfect!"

Six

◇

"Carrot sticks for breakfast?" Steven asked Saturday morning as he entered the kitchen.

Jessica was sitting at the kitchen table munching on her tenth carrot stick of the morning. "Carrots are very good for you. They're full of vitamin A," she informed her brother. She picked up a piece of carrot and offered it to him.

"Thanks," he said, grimacing. "I think I'll stick with cereal."

Jessica reached for another carrot stick and moved it slowly back and forth, following it closely with her eyes.

Steven sat down at the kitchen table and watched her with amusement. "Jessica, can I ask you something?"

"Sure." Jessica held the carrot stick at arm's length and pulled it toward her until it nearly touched her nose.

"Why are you trying to hypnotize yourself with a carrot stick?"

Jessica took a bite out of the carrot and smiled. "I'm improving my vision, if you must know."

Steven crossed his arms over his chest. "Yeah, right. If you don't want to tell me, fine."

"But it's true!"

"After you're done working on your vision, maybe you should try working on your brain," Steven snorted.

Jessica reached for the last of her carrot sticks and jumped to her feet. "I don't care what you say, Steven. I know it's working."

She closed one eye, opened it, then closed the other. The morning newspaper lay on the table. The words *Sweet Valley Tribune* at the top of the page were perfectly clear. Of course, they were the biggest letters on the page, but that was OK. At least it was a start. At this rate, she would be completely cured by Monday.

That afternoon, the Unicorns came over to Jessica's house for their special meeting. They decided to sit on the Wakefields' backyard patio while they worked.

Janet Howell settled into a lounge chair. She was wearing a pair of mirror sunglasses. "Is everybody ready? Belinda said she'd be a few minutes late, but the rest of us might as well get started. We have a lot of planning to do if we're going to have our fundraiser in time to be included in Elizabeth's article. By the way, Jessica, where *is* Elizabeth, anyway?"

"She's over at Amy Sutton's," Jessica replied as she picked up yet another carrot. "She should be back in a little while."

"Good," Janet said. "I was hoping we could tell her about our idea." Janet pulled down her sunglasses and peered at Jessica. "Why are you holding all those carrot sticks? Are you on a new diet?"

"I just happen to like carrots, that's all," Jessica said defensively. "They're very good for you, you know."

"Can I have one?" Ellen asked.

"No," Jessica said, "I need them all."

"Some hostess *you* are." Ellen tossed her head.

Just then, Belinda appeared at the sliding doors that opened onto the patio. "Sorry I'm late, everybody," she said. "I was baby-sitting my baby brother all morning."

"Oh, he's so cute! You guys should see him!" Ellen cooed.

"He really is adorable. But I'd hate to have to share anything with a brother or a sister. I'm much happier being an only child." Lila sighed contentedly.

"If we could get back to business, please," Janet said in her bossiest voice. "I've got a wonderful idea for a way to raise money."

"Money for what?" Lila asked as she examined a nail.

"For our *good deed*," Janet reminded her impatiently.

"Oh, yes." Lila laughed. "I forgot."

"My older brother went on a walk-a-thon a few months ago to help raise money for a charity," Janet continued. "So I started thinking, why couldn't the Unicorns sponsor a walk-a-thon of our own?"

"How exactly does a walk-a-thon work?" Ellen asked.

"Each person who participates in the walk gets people to contribute a certain amount of money for each mile. My brother got ten people to sponsor him. Each one pledged a dollar to the charity for every mile he was able to walk. He walked ten miles, so he raised a hundred dollars in one afternoon!"

"Wow!" Belinda cried. "Think how much money *we* could raise!"

"There might even be money left over for curling irons!" Ellen said hopefully.

"Wait a minute." Lila frowned in distaste. "Does this mean *we'd* have to walk all day? For *miles*?"

"Not necessarily," Janet said thoughtfully. "We could get other students to do the walking. The Unicorns could just organize the event."

Lila nodded approvingly.

Jessica swallowed the last of her carrots. She hadn't been paying much attention to Janet. The truth was, she was much too worried about her own problem to care whether or not the school got a new, odor-free encyclopedia set. But she did have a suggestion.

"I've got an idea," she said quietly.

"What, Jessica?" Janet asked.

"How about a *skate*-a-thon instead of a walk-a-thon? We could hold it at the skating rink."

"That's a wonderful idea!" Mary exclaimed. "Everybody loves to skate!"

"And people could pledge money for each hour that someone skates," Janet mused. "All we have to do is get the owner of Skateland to donate the rink for a few hours."

"But Skateland is closed for remodeling," Ellen pointed out. "It's not due to reopen until next Saturday."

"Oh, I'd forgotten about that," Jessica admitted.

"You know, my father knows the owner," Belinda said. "I could ask him to call for us. Maybe he would agree to reopen a day early. After all, it's for a good cause."

"Perfect!" Janet smiled. "If your dad can arrange for the place, that will be even less work for us. Now, all we need to do is make a few posters to put up around school. The skaters will collect their pledge money after the skate-a-thon and give it to us. Then we present the money to the library, and before you know it, we'll be on the cover of the *Sweet Valley Tribune!*"

"How can we be sure Elizabeth will write about us?" Ellen asked.

"Oh, she will," Janet said confidently.

"I will what?" Elizabeth stepped out onto the patio. Amy followed close behind.

"When you hear about the good deed the Unicorns have planned, you're sure to feature us in your article about students who make a difference," Janet explained.

Elizabeth and Amy smiled at each other.

"We're going to help the library." Lila smiled grandly.

"How do you plan to do that?" Amy asked skeptically. "By painting the library purple?"

"We're organizing a fundraiser," Jessica said, defensively.

"I'll believe it when I see it!" Amy rolled her eyes.

"We're buying the library a new encyclopedia set," Janet snapped.

Elizabeth took one look at Amy and burst out laughing. She glanced around at the angry Unicorns. "I'm sorry, you guys," she said apologetically. "It's just that the idea of you—" She paused, looked at Amy, and laughed again. "Come on, Amy," she said at last. "I can't stand it anymore!"

Janet watched as Amy and Elizabeth went back into the house. "Jessica," Janet said, a determined gleam in her eye, "before this is over, we're going to teach that sister of yours a lesson!"

At one o'clock on Monday afternoon, Jessica and Elizabeth waited outside Sweet Valley Middle School for Mrs. Wakefield to pick them up.

"I like getting out of school early," Jessica said, leaning against the flagpole on the front lawn. "But I wish we didn't have to go to the eye doctor."

"Cheer up, Jess," Elizabeth said. "You said you thought your eyes seemed a little better. Maybe you won't need glasses after all."

"I've stared at that pencil so long, I'm starting

to get cross-eyed," Jessica moaned. "And I've eaten so many carrots, I think my skin's turning orange." She took a step closer to Elizabeth. "Tell me the truth, Elizabeth. Do you think I'm turning orange?"

Elizabeth pursed her lips. "Maybe just a little."

"I knew it!" Jessica fumed. "I'll be the only girl in school with orange skin, crossed eyes, and glasses! The Unicorns will dump me for sure. Not to mention Aaron!"

At that moment Mrs. Wakefield drove up the broad driveway that curved in front of the school and tapped lightly on her horn.

Jessica looked at her twin and sighed. "I guess we might as well get this over with."

The girls climbed into the car. All the way to the eye doctor's office, Jessica stared gloomily out of the window. She didn't speak until they were sitting in the waiting room.

"Elizabeth?" Jessica whispered. She glanced over at Mrs. Wakefield, who was filling out forms for the receptionist. "When the doctor tests my eyes, do you think there's a way to cheat a little?"

"Cheat? I doubt it, Jess."

But when the nurse called Jessica into the examination room a few minutes later, Jessica was determined to try anything, even cheating. She was convinced it was her only real hope of passing the eye examination. In her heart she knew that the carrots and the pencil exercise hadn't changed a thing.

Jessica sat in a big, padded examination chair and waited for the doctor to arrive. It was only a minute before Dr. Cruz came in. He was a serious-looking man with dark hair and big, thick black glasses that made his eyes look huge.

Well, I won't get any sympathy from him, Jessica thought dejectedly.

"Jessica Wakefield?" Dr. Cruz asked, reading her name from her chart.

"Yes," Jessica answered brightly. "I don't know why I'm here, doctor. My eyes are just fine, but my mother is always worrying about silly health things that turn out to be nothing."

"I don't think your eyes are silly, Jessica," Dr. Cruz said seriously.

"Yes, but I can see fine. I can see you, and I can see that stool over there." Jessica glanced around the room. "I can even see that picture of a dog on your desk. Is that your dog?"

"Actually, no," Dr. Cruz said. "That's my grandson."

"Oh." Jessica colored. "I'm sorry."

"There's nothing to be sorry about. It's not your fault that you couldn't see the picture clearly. It *will* be your fault if you do nothing to correct the problem."

Jessica sighed. This doctor sounded exactly like a teacher.

"Now, I'm going to turn off the lights." Dr. Cruz touched a switch on the wall, and the room went dark. Then a small circle of bright light appeared on the wall in front of Jessica. "I'm going to show you what will look like the letter *E*. I want you to tell me which way the arms of the letter are aimed. Just point with your hand, or you can say 'left' or 'right,' or 'up' or 'down.' Do you understand?"

Jessica nodded. The first image of the letter was easy to see. "Right," she said confidently. But the next image was smaller and seemed a little blurry. Jessica squinted. "Left," she said at last.

"Don't squint, Jessica. Just look normally," Dr. Cruz instructed.

"I normally squint," Jessica replied. "I don't *have* to, I just like to squint." The next image was smaller still, and even with squinting, Jessica could not be sure which way it pointed. "Um, up?"

"Sorry, Jessica," Dr. Cruz said. "Now, I'm going to cover one eye." He blocked her right eye with a sort of patch. "Can you see it now?"

"Yes! It's down!" Jessica answered happily.

"Correct." He changed the image again, and this time he covered her left eye with the patch.

"Left," Jessica answered correctly. "Didn't I tell you? I can see just fine!"

"Yes, each eye *is* fine by itself. But together, the eyes don't focus very well." Dr. Cruz looked at her thoughtfully. "I have to do some more tests, but my guess is I'll have good news for you. You may not have to wear glasses—"

"Great!"

"—for more than a couple of months."

Twenty minutes later, Jessica walked back into the waiting room and dropped gloomily into a chair next to Elizabeth.

"What did Dr. Cruz say, honey?" Mrs. Wakefield asked gently.

"He said my life is over." Jessica sighed.

Seven

◇

"What do you mean, *you* don't need glasses?" Jessica shouted at Elizabeth. "If I need glasses, you must need them, too!"

Dr. Cruz had asked Mrs. Wakefield and Jessica into his office after he had finished examining Elizabeth. He smiled consolingly at Jessica. "Just because you're twins doesn't necessarily mean your eyesight is precisely the same," he explained.

"But it's just not fair!" Jessica wailed.

"Actually, you should be relieved we caught the problem as early as we did," Dr. Cruz said. "The muscles in your eyes can be strengthened, but only if you wear glasses for a few months."

"A few months! It might as well be forever," Jessica cried.

"If you don't wear the glasses now, your eyes will only get worse," Dr. Cruz warned. He handed Mrs. Wakefield a slip of paper. "Here's the prescription for Jessica's lenses. There's an excellent lab at the mall that can fill simple eyeglass prescriptions in one hour."

"One hour?" Jessica echoed pathetically. "Can't we go somewhere where it takes a little longer? Like a few years?"

In spite of Jessica's protests, Mrs. Wakefield drove the twins straight to the mall from Dr. Cruz's office. When they reached the entrance to the Valley Vision Center, Jessica paused and glanced over her shoulder nervously.

"Elizabeth," she said. "Promise me you'll keep your eyes open for anyone we know. If you see somebody from school, just signal."

"Don't worry," Elizabeth reassured her. "I'll stand here by the doorway and be your lookout."

The Vision Center seemed alien to Jessica. The employees were all wearing white lab coats, and they all wore glasses. It was the only store she had ever been in where she didn't have the urge to buy a single thing.

Mrs. Wakefield reached over to a display rack and pulled down a pair of light pink frames. "Here," she said. "Try these on, Jessica."

Jessica glanced over at Elizabeth, who nodded. "It's all clear, Jess," she called.

Reluctantly, Jessica slipped on the glasses. They felt very strange. Her nose itched, and no matter where she looked, she always saw the edges of the frames. It was like having two tiny windows on her cheeks.

Then she noticed something else that was odd. "There's no glass in these glasses," she observed.

"That's why Dr. Cruz gave you a prescription," Mrs. Wakefield said. "You pick out the frames you like, and then they grind your lenses here to match your prescription."

"Those look cute on you, Jessica," Elizabeth called from her station in the doorway.

Jessica stepped over to a mirror. "Ugh," she groaned, grimacing at her reflection. All she could see were the pink glasses. It was as though her face, the Jessica she was used to seeing, had vanished.

"Hi. My name is Julie. May I help you find some frames?" asked a petite, auburn-haired woman in a white coat. She was wearing big red glasses. "Is there a particular style you're looking for?"

"Yes." Jessica yanked the frames off her face impatiently. "Something invisible."

Julie took the frames from Jessica and smiled pleasantly. "I'll bet this is your first pair of glasses."

"And my last, I hope," Jessica said.

"You have such lovely blue eyes. Why don't you try these on?" Julie handed Jessica a pair of glasses from a different display case. The thin plastic frames were a pretty soft violet color.

Jessica slipped the frames on and scowled at her image in the mirror.

"I think those glasses make your eyes look even bluer," Julie commented.

"They are very attractive on you, Jessica," Mrs. Wakefield agreed.

"Let's see, Jess!" Elizabeth said.

Jessica turned to face her twin.

"They look great on you!" Elizabeth said enthusiastically. "I wish I could get a pair."

Jessica gave her a doubtful look and handed the frames to Julie. "How about those instead?" Jessica asked, pointing to a pair of wire-rimmed frames.

For the next hour, Jessica tried on frame after frame. Some, she had to admit, looked better than others. But they all suffered from the same basic problem. "No matter which pair I try on, I *still* look as if I'm wearing glasses," she complained.

"You *are* wearing glasses," Julie pointed out wearily as she returned yet another pair of frames to the display case. She looked Jessica straight in the eye. "Trust me on this. When I first got glasses, I was fourteen years old, and I thought my world was coming to an end. But now I love wearing them."

Jessica stared at Julie's red frames. Somehow, on Julie, they looked just right. But when Jessica tried on a similar pair, she had looked absolutely hideous. "Sure," Jessica said, "on *you*, glasses look good."

"And they will on you, too," Julie assured her confidently. "It just takes a while to get used to them."

"After a while you won't even notice you're wearing them!" Mrs. Wakefield added.

"*I* may not notice," Jessica replied grimly, "but everyone else will!"

Mrs. Wakefield checked her watch. "Are there any frames you like better than the others, honey? It's really time to decide."

Jessica shrugged. "I look equally ugly in all of them."

"I like the light violet frames you tried on at the beginning," Elizabeth volunteered. "You always wear at least one purple thing, so they would go with everything."

"I liked them, too," Mrs. Wakefield agreed.

"So did I." Julie nodded. "They complimented your features nicely."

"Fine," Jessica said. She sounded resigned. "If that's what you all like, that's what I'll get." She sighed. "It's just too bad you guys don't have to wear them."

While they waited for Jessica's glasses to be made, Mrs. Wakefield took the twins shopping. She told them that they could each pick out something they liked at Kendall's, one of the twins' favorite stores.

Normally, Jessica would have been thrilled at the chance to pick out a new outfit, but today she wandered listlessly past the clothes racks.

"Can't you find anything you like, Jessica?" Mrs. Wakefield asked, sorting through a rack of blouses.

Jessica shook her head slowly. She knew her mother was trying to cheer her up, and she was grateful, but there really wasn't any point in it. She was beyond being cheered up. "It won't matter what I wear, Mom," she said, flatly. "All anyone's going to notice are my glasses. You can't exactly camouflage them."

"Jessica! Look what I found!" Elizabeth dashed over to her sister. She held up a dark purple skirt with a matching top.

For a brief moment, Jessica's eyes lit up. "Lila and I were fighting over that same outfit the last time we were here! We both loved it, but neither of us had any money. Lila was going to charge it to her father's account, but he was away on a business trip and the clerk needed his OK."

"Well, you'd better grab it fast because it's the last one in the store." Elizabeth winked at Mrs. Wakefield.

Jessica fingered the purple fabric wistfully. "It *is* awfully cute," she said quietly.

"Great!" Elizabeth thrust the hanger into Jessica's hand.

But I still say, no one will notice my outfit once they see my geeky glasses, Jessica told herself. She held the purple top in front of her and gazed at herself in a full-length mirror. She looked really good. Aaron would be very impressed. *If only I didn't have to ruin the effect with glasses!* she thought sadly.

Then an idea struck her. Jessica smiled deviously at her reflection. Just because she had glasses didn't mean she had to *wear* them!

"You're right, Elizabeth," she said happily. "I think I'll take this outfit!"

After Elizabeth picked out a blouse she liked, Mrs. Wakefield went to the register to pay for the twins' new clothes. Jessica pulled Elizabeth aside, out of Mrs. Wakefield's hearing range.

"You won't tell a soul about my glasses, will you, Elizabeth?" she whispered.

"Of course not. But people are going to know about them soon enough, Jess."

"I know," Jessica replied. "I just want to break it to them gently."

Elizabeth wrinkled her brow. "But Dr. Cruz said—"

"I know what Dr. Cruz said. But let me handle this my way, OK?" Jessica gave her twin a pleading look. "Please, Lizzie."

Elizabeth hesitated. "All right."

Jessica glanced back at the full-length mirror and smiled triumphantly. She was going to look great in her new purple dress—*without* her glasses!

"Why, Jessica! You look wonderful!" Mr. Wakefield exclaimed the next morning when Jessica entered the kitchen wearing her new glasses.

"Thanks, Dad. You already told me that last night."

"Well, I *mean* it. You look very sophisticated," Mr. Wakefield insisted.

"I'm not sure they're really helping my eyes, though," Jessica remarked. "The frames keep getting in the way whenever I try to look at anything. Maybe we should take these back and exchange them for another pair."

"You'll get used to them in no time," Mr. Wakefield assured her. He took a sip from his cup of coffee. "In a day or two, you won't even know you have them on."

Just then, Steven walked into the kitchen. He took one look at Jessica, and his mouth dropped open.

"You've already seen your sister's new glasses, Steven," Mr. Wakefield said sternly. "No comments are necessary."

"Close your mouth, Steven," Jessica said. "You're letting in flies."

"It's just that you look—"

"Steven!" Mr. Wakefield warned, shooting him a look that clearly meant *Be careful what you say*.

"—great," Steven finished. "You look great, Jess. Really." He headed for the refrigerator, but even with his back to her, Jessica was certain her brother was laughing under his breath.

"Are you ready, Jessica?" Elizabeth asked, poking her head into the kitchen.

"As ready as I'll ever be." Jessica grabbed her backpack and followed her sister outside.

"I thought you were going to wear your new outfit," Elizabeth said as the girls walked down the driveway.

"I decided to save it for my date with Aaron." Jessica paused and glanced up and down the street. "Do you see anyone?" she asked anxiously. "Anyone from school?"

Elizabeth smiled understandingly. "Nope. The coast is clear."

Together the girls began walking toward school. "It's true what everyone's been saying about your glasses," Elizabeth remarked as they reached the end of the block. "In a few days you won't even know they're there."

Jessica didn't answer. She had stopped a few feet back.

"Jessica?" Elizabeth spun around. "Your glasses!" she exclaimed. "Where are they?"

"I put them in my backpack," Jessica explained.

"But you're supposed—" Elizabeth began.

"I know what I'm supposed to do, Elizabeth. But I have to get used to the idea first. It's like breaking in a new pair of shoes. Trust me, OK?"

"Well," Elizabeth said slowly, "OK."

"And you won't tell anyone about my glasses?"

Elizabeth nodded. "But you'll start wearing them soon, right?"

"You're the best sister in the world, Elizabeth," Jessica replied, avoiding her question.

"I just think—"

"Say, isn't that Mandy Miller up ahead?" Jessica interrupted, pointing down the street. "Mandy!" she called.

Mandy turned and waved. "Jessica!" she cried,

obviously surprised. She ran back to join the twins. "Were you calling *me*?"

"Sure," Jessica replied breezily. "Why not?"

"I don't know," Mandy answered, falling into step beside the twins. "Usually you act as if I'm invisible."

But Jessica didn't respond. They had reached school, and she had spotted Lila and was waving her over.

"See what I mean?" Mandy turned to Elizabeth. She adjusted a strap of her bright yellow suspenders and shrugged good-naturedly.

"Jessica has a lot on her mind," Elizabeth said apologetically.

"What?" Jessica asked when she heard her name mentioned. "Oh, sorry, Mandy. Were you talking to me?"

Mandy opened her mouth to speak just as Lila joined the group.

"There you are!" Lila cried. "Janet's been driving me crazy ever since I got to school. Yesterday, Mary and Belinda made posters for our fund-raiser, and now you and I are supposed to hang them up."

"What fund-raiser?" Mandy asked curiously.

"They made dozens of them, too," Lila continued, ignoring Mandy's question. "How are we supposed to find time to hang them all?"

Jessica looked at Mandy and smiled sweetly. "Don't worry, Lila. I think I've found the solution to our problem!"

"How's the article for the *Tribune* coming?" Amy asked Elizabeth as they walked toward the cafeteria at lunchtime.

"I interviewed the Chess Club about their project," Elizabeth replied. "But somehow I don't think the story is going to be enough."

"Enough?"

"It's just that playing chess by mail isn't very exciting. And I can't see how it benefits the community. I want this article to be really special."

Near the entrance to the cafeteria, they saw Mandy Miller carefully taping a colorful, hand-painted poster to the wall.

"A *skate-a-thon*?" Amy read aloud. "What's this?"

" 'Help Raise Money for the Unicorn Library Fund,' " Elizabeth read. " 'Friday, six to ten P.M. Collect pledges for each hour you skate and help Sweet Valley Middle School buy a new encyclopedia set.' "

Amy giggled. "They're actually going through with this?"

"Why are *you* hanging this up, Mandy?" Elizabeth asked.

"Oh, I hung up all the posters," Mandy replied proudly. "I did it as a favor to Jessica."

"That was awfully nice of you. I hope she appreciates it." Elizabeth knew that her twin sometimes took advantage of people.

"I don't mind," Mandy responded brightly. "After all, it's for a good cause."

"I suppose," Elizabeth said dubiously.

"Looks great, Mandy!" Jessica called, heading toward them with Janet, Ellen, and Lila in tow.

"What do you think?" Janet asked Elizabeth.

"Well, it's a good idea," Elizabeth began hesitantly. "But—"

"But what?" Lila demanded.

"But we'll believe it when we see it," Amy finished.

"It's just hard to imagine the Unicorns pulling this off, that's all," Elizabeth said. "Fund-raisers are a lot of work." Even if the Unicorns really meant well, and she doubted they did, Elizabeth was certain they would make a mess of things, as always.

"Just save some room in your article for us," Janet replied.

"So she can tell everyone how you guys messed things up?" Amy teased.

Janet smiled confidently. "Just be sure to bring your notebook Friday night, Elizabeth," she responded with a cool smile. "I think you're going to be *very* surprised."

Eight

◇

"Jessica, it's been two days, and you're still not wearing your glasses!" Elizabeth cried in exasperation.

"Sh!" Jessica put her finger to her lips and closed her bedroom door. "I wear them, Lizzie," she protested. "I just don't wear them all the time." With an impish smile, she removed her glasses and dropped them onto her desk.

"Yes, but you only wear them around the house when Mom and Dad might see you."

"So? That's a start," Jessica replied airily. "I'm still getting used to them." She held her hand in front of her face and examined her nails. "I wonder if I should wear nail polish on my date Sunday?"

"*I* wonder if you should wear your glasses."

"*Please*, Elizabeth!" Jessica groaned. "Did you happen to see Aaron today?"

"No. Why?"

"No reason." Jessica closed her eyes and sighed. "It's just that he looked extra cute today."

"Gee, I didn't think that was possible," Elizabeth joked.

Just then, there was a knock on the Jessica's door. "May I come in, girls?" Mrs. Wakefield called from the hallway.

"Quick! My glasses!" Jessica dashed for her desk and grabbed them just as Mrs. Wakefield opened the door.

"Is it dinnertime already, Mom?" Jessica asked casually. With her back to her mother, she slipped on her glasses.

"Not yet," Mrs. Wakefield replied. "Your dad and I were just thinking it might be fun for the family to take in an early movie."

"Tonight?" Elizabeth asked in surprise. "On a school night?"

"That new movie you kids have been dying to see is at Valley Cinema. We thought the theater might not be as crowded as it will be this weekend," Mrs. Wakefield said.

"*Tale of Love II* is here?" Elizabeth asked excitedly.

Mrs. Wakefield nodded. "Besides, it'll be fun for Jessica to try out her new glasses. The screen will be so much clearer!"

"I have a lot of homework, Mom," Jessica said suddenly.

"Just those four math problems," Elizabeth reminded her. "I'll help you with them before dinner."

Jessica shot her a warning look.

"Great," Mrs. Wakefield said. "Plan on leaving right after dinner."

"What about the dishes?" Jessica asked.

Mrs. Wakefield laughed. "They can wait, just this once!"

"Thanks a whole lot, Elizabeth!" Jessica snapped as soon as Mrs. Wakefield closed the door. "Now I've got to go out in public, and the whole planet will see my geeky glasses!"

"But it'll be dark in the theater," Elizabeth pointed out.

"What about going in and out of the theater?"

"Don't worry, Jess," Elizabeth assured her. "It's a school night, after all. What are the chances that anyone we know will be there?"

Jessica stared at the ceiling and groaned. When it came to her glasses, she wasn't in the mood to take any chances at all.

*   *   *

Jessica slumped in her seat and prayed for the opening credits of the movie to begin. *So far, so good*, she thought. The theater was only half full, and most of the people there were high school students and adults.

Steven was sitting next to Jessica in the aisle seat. He shoved a bucket of popcorn toward her.

"No, thanks," she muttered.

"How come you're sitting like that?" he asked. "Are you planning to take a nap?"

"I'm just getting comfortable," Jessica snapped.

Suddenly the lights in the theater dimmed, and the movie screen flickered to life. *At last*, Jessica thought. *Now I can relax and enjoy the movie in peace.* She sat up in her chair and adjusted her glasses. As much as she hated to admit it, the screen did seem a lot clearer. And it was nice not to have to squint.

As the music swelled and the opening credits to *Tale of Love II* rolled past on the big screen, Jessica felt a surge of excitement. She'd been on the edge of her seat for most of *Tale of Love*, anxious to see if the stars would end up together. She hoped this sequel would be just as exciting and romantic. She reached for Steven's bucket of popcorn and retrieved a big handful.

"Jessica? *Jessica Wakefield?*"

Jessica froze, her popcorn-filled fist in midair. She knew that voice, all too well.

"*Jessica?*" whispered a dark figure in the aisle, barely visible in the flickering light. "It's me, Lila. Am I crazy, or are you wearing *glasses*?"

Jessica felt her heart jump into her throat. She was doomed.

"Jess?" Lila persisted.

"Quiet!" someone nearby scolded.

Jessica felt paralyzed. No matter how long she ignored Lila, she wasn't going to go away. But Jessica couldn't bear to face her, either.

At last she dropped her handful of popcorn back into Steven's bucket and stood up. "I'll be right back," she whispered to her parents.

"It *is* you!" Lila gloated as Jessica joined her in the aisle. "Isn't it a little early for Halloween?"

"Would you *please* shut up?" someone hissed.

"Come on, Lila," Jessica whispered, pushing her toward the exit. "Let's talk outside."

Jessica yanked off her glasses and stalked ahead. Except for an usher, the lobby was deserted.

"What are you doing here, anyway?" Jessica demanded.

"My dad just got back from a business trip, and he was feeling guilty about not having seen me in a while," Lila explained. "I talked him into bring- ing me here so we could spend some time together." She reached for the glasses in Jessica's hand and tried them on. "Are these yours?"

Jessica chewed on her lower lip. She had to think fast. "No, they're my mom's," she lied. "I was just trying them on."

"I didn't know your mom wore glasses," Lila said doubtfully.

"She just got them."

Lila handed the glasses back to Jessica and crossed her arms over her chest. "I can tell when you're lying, Jessica Wakefield."

"I'm not lying," Jessica said as convincingly as she could.

Lila tossed her hair back over her shoulder. "Where were you Monday afternoon, anyway?"

"I had an appointment," Jessica answered automatically. "A doctor's appointment."

"Eye doctor, if you ask me," Lila said knowingly. "Those frames are too small for your mom."

Jessica stared desperately at the floor. She knew Lila had her cornered. "All right," she admitted. "I *did* get glasses. But I only have to wear them for a tiny amount of time, and then my eyes will be back to normal. And nobody has to know about it, Lila, if you can just keep your big mouth shut!"

"*Moi?*" Lila fluttered her lashes, looking very innocent. "Who would *I* tell?"

"Everyone in the Sweet Valley phone book," Jessica retorted. There was no way to keep Lila quiet now. No way, unless . . . "Lila!" Jessica exclaimed. "Remember that great purple outfit we saw at Kendall's a few days ago? The one we both wanted so badly to buy?"

Lila nodded. "I'm going to ask my dad to buy it for me this weekend." Lila's father spoiled her by buying her anything she wanted.

"Too bad there was only one left." Jessica shook her head. "I bought it Monday afternoon to wear on my date with Aaron. Of course, I might be willing to give it to you if—"

"If I keep my mouth shut about your glasses?" Lila guessed.

"Exactly. But you can't tell a soul."

"Ever?" Lila asked.

"*Ever*," Jessica told her adamantly.

Lila hesitated.

"I'll give you my new purple earrings, too," Jessica added reluctantly. "I've only worn them twice."

"It's a deal!" Lila agreed. "Will you bring them to school with you tomorrow?"

Jessica nodded. "Now let's get back to the movie. My family's going to wonder what happened to me."

"Don't forget to bring my outfit," Lila whispered as they walked back down the aisle to their seats.

Jessica didn't answer. She returned to her seat, put her glasses back on, and tried to watch the movie. But when it was all over, she wasn't even sure what it had been all about. She supposed she would just have to wait for the video.

"Here it is, Lila." Jessica stood in front of Lila's locker on Friday morning. She reached into her backpack and handed Lila a brown paper bag. "Now, don't forget your end of the bargain."

"Where are my earrings?" Lila demanded.

Jessica made a face. She had been hoping Lila would forget about them. "Oh, all right." Jessica reached into her backpack again. "Here."

Lila held one of the earrings up to her ear. "What do you think?"

"You have excellent taste," Jessica observed dryly.

"I've been thinking, Jess," Lila said as she opened the brown bag and inspected its contents. "There's one other thing that would make this outfit complete."

"What?"

"Those glasses of yours!" Lila burst into laughter.

"You're a real comedian, Lila," Jessica growled.

She glanced around the hallway. "Keep your voice down, will you?"

"Don't be so paranoid. No one heard me."

"Well, keep it that way," Jessica said.

"Jessica! I'm really hurt," Lila said. "Your little secret's safe with me! And if you can't trust me, who can you trust?"

"Nobody," Jessica answered under her breath as she started down the hallway. She knew she couldn't buy Lila's silence forever. Right now, all she wanted was to get through her date on Sunday without Aaron knowing about her glasses. Maybe once he got to know her a little better, he wouldn't mind so much if she had to wear glasses for a while.

"Oh, Jessica!" Lila called.

Jessica spun around. "What?"

"Would you mind coming back here for a minute?" Lila's silky-sweet voice made Jessica want to scream.

"What do you want?" Jessica asked, walking back to Lila's locker. "It's almost time for homeroom."

"My arm is really sore this morning. I must have slept on it wrong. Would you mind carrying my books for me?"

Jessica looked at Lila in disbelief. "Carry your books?" she repeated. "Are you crazy?"

Lila simply smiled.

The hall was growing emptier by the minute. Jessica glanced at the clock on the wall. "Oh, all right," she cried. "Give me your stupid books!"

Lila led the way down the hall with Jessica trailing behind, loaded down with books. "I'm not your personal slave, Lila," Jessica said under her breath.

But for the time being, Jessica knew that that was exactly what she was.

"Why are you carrying Lila's lunch tray for her?" Ellen asked as Jessica and Lila sat down at the Unicorner at noon.

"It's my good deed for the day," Jessica snapped.

"Speaking of good deeds," Janet said, "things are going very well on the skate-a-thon. Belinda's father called the manager of Skateland and confirmed the use of the rink tonight. Sweet Valley Middle School will have it all to ourselves!"

"And lots of people have already signed up to skate," Mary added. "With all the pledges they're getting, we'll make more than enough money to pay for the encyclopedias!"

"Has anyone here gotten pledges?" Belinda asked.

The Unicorns looked at each other in surprise.

"Why would *we* do that?" Ellen asked. "We're organizing. We don't actually have to skate."

"But it sounds like fun," Belinda protested.

"Skating for four whole hours?" Lila grimaced. "Our job is only to collect money from everyone after the skate-a-thon is over."

Jessica was just about to speak when she noticed Aaron and Jake approaching the Unicorner. "Aaron!" she exclaimed.

"Hi, Jess," he said, glancing uncomfortably at the table of gawking Unicorns. "I wanted to make sure you were still planning on going to Sunday's game with me."

"Are you kidding?" Lila laughed. "It's all she's been talking about for *days!*"

Jessica shot Lila a fierce look, but Lila just pointed to her eyes with her index finger and gave Jessica a knowing smile.

"What time is the game?" Jessica asked, trying to ignore Lila.

"Two o'clock. We'll pick you up at one, OK?"

"Great," Jessica replied.

"Jessica?" Lila said sweetly.

Jessica sighed. "What is it now, Lila?"

"I'm done with my lunch."

"So?" Jessica clenched her teeth. Aaron looked at Lila curiously.

"So would you please take away my tray now?"

Several of the Unicorns stared at Lila in astonishment.

Jessica gave Aaron an embarrassed smile. "I'll be right there, Lila," she said meekly.

Aaron looked from Lila to Jessica and back again. "See you, Jessica," he said, shaking his head.

As soon as Aaron was out of earshot, Jessica turned to Lila. "I hope you're satisfied, Lila."

Lila shrugged. "Can I have your chocolate cake, Jessica?" she asked. "I'm awfully hungry."

Jessica picked up the plate with her cake on it. For a brief moment she considered throwing it at Lila. But she remembered the pair of glasses stashed inside her backpack and restrained herself. She could either be Lila's slave for a while, or a geek for life.

"Here you go," she said, passing the plate across the table.

Nine

◇

"Elizabeth! Can't you hurry up a little?"

Jessica stood outside the bathroom that evening, her hands on her hips, watching impatiently while Elizabeth carefully combed her hair. "You're going to make me late."

"That would be a change." Elizabeth shook her head. "*Me* make *you* late? Besides, what's the big hurry? This skate-a-thon is supposed to go on for four hours. Are you afraid the whole thing will flop before we can get there?"

"Very funny, Elizabeth." Jessica turned away and headed down the stairs. "Just you wait, big sister," she whispered to herself. "We'll see if you're still laughing soon."

Jessica was halfway down the stairs when the doorbell rang. When she opened the front door, she saw Amy Sutton holding a notebook with a pencil stuck in the wire binder.

"Hi, Amy," Jessica said. "Come on in. Elizabeth is still upstairs."

"I am not," Elizabeth called, coming down the stairs. "I'm all ready. I'm sorry to keep you both waiting, but I thought I should look my best to cover the Unicorns' latest disaster."

Amy laughed. "Elizabeth, we have to keep an open mind. After all, the Unicorns don't *always* mess up when they try to organize things." She paused and put one finger to her chin, pretending to search her memory. "Hm. On second thought, I guess they *do* always mess things up."

"You're both hilarious," Jessica said sarcastically. "Besides," she added, casting a sidelong glance at her twin, "I'm sure Ellen and Lila managed to take care of all those little last-minute problems."

"Last-minute problems?" Elizabeth echoed, exchanging a knowing look with Amy. "What last-minute problems?"

"Nothing. Nothing at all," Jessica said quickly. "Ellen and Lila are perfectly capable of—"

"Sure," Amy interrupted, barely concealing a

smirk. "Ellen and Lila are real geniuses when it comes to organization."

"Well, let's get going," Elizabeth said. "At least this will be good for a laugh." She led the way out the door.

Suddenly, Jessica snapped her fingers. "I forgot something!"

"What?" Elizabeth asked.

"Um—um, I forgot my lip gloss. You two go on ahead. I'll catch up."

Jessica dashed back into the house and grabbed the phone in the den. She quickly dialed a number. "Hi, Janet?" she said breathlessly. "It's me, Jessica. We're on our way, so make sure everything is ready!"

Jessica caught up with Amy and Elizabeth about halfway to the skating rink. As the three girls pulled up on their bikes outside Skateland, they noticed most of the Unicorns, led by Janet and Lila, walking out to meet them. No one looked very happy.

"Hi, everyone," Jessica said brightly.

"Hello, Jessica," Janet said in a subdued voice. "Hi, Elizabeth. Hi, Amy."

"What's the matter, Janet?" Jessica demanded. "You guys look depressed."

"Well . . ." Ellen said. "It's about the skate-a-thon."

"Everything's OK, isn't it?" Jessica asked nervously.

"Well . . ." Ellen shifted uneasily. "Most of it's OK."

"There's this one tiny little problem," Lila said.

"A tiny problem?" Jessica echoed. She shot a glance at Elizabeth and Amy. They were grinning smugly.

"You might as well tell us," Elizabeth said.

"Yes, we *are* reporters, after all," Amy added. "We'll find out sooner or later. Just exactly how have the Unicorns messed up *this* time?"

"It's not really our fault," Ellen protested. "When the owner of Skateland agreed to reopen a day early for us, we just assumed . . ."

"How were we to know?" Lila interjected, shrugging her shoulders.

"Know what?" Elizabeth demanded in exasperation.

Janet stared down at the ground. "While Skateland was closed for remodeling, all the skates were sent out to be cleaned and repaired. They won't be back until tomorrow. The owner thought everyone was bringing his or her own skates. He *says* he told us, but . . ."

"You mean you're holding a skate-a-thon—" Elizabeth began.

"—without any skates?" Amy finished.

The two friends looked at each other and began to laugh hysterically.

"It doesn't matter," Lila said defensively. "We've figured out a way to make it all work."

Elizabeth could barely speak through her laughter. "H-H-How?"

"We'll all just *pretend* we have skates," Janet explained. "Lila, Ellen, show them."

As Elizabeth and Amy watched, helpless with laughter, Lila and Ellen began to pretend they were skating. Gliding forward on one foot, then the other, they swung their arms by their sides in a solemn pantomime.

"Look! I can skate backward!" Ellen turned around and began to move backward.

Elizabeth and Amy doubled over with laughter as tears streamed down their cheeks.

"This will go down in history as the greatest Unicorn foul-up ever," Elizabeth pronounced when she finally caught her breath. "Come on, Amy, let's go inside."

"I can't, Elizabeth," Amy protested. "I'm in pain from laughing so hard!"

"We have to," Elizabeth said, struggling to put on a serious face. "After all, we *are* reporters."

Elizabeth and Amy headed toward the front door of the skating rink while the Unicorns trooped along behind.

The moment Elizabeth entered the rink, her jaw dropped open in amazement. The walls were hung with professional-looking posters explaining the skate-a-thon. Clusters of brightly colored helium balloons hung from the ceiling, giving the whole room a festive look. At a booth in one corner, two of the Unicorns were busily writing down the names of the skaters and the amounts of their pledges. A chalkboard had been set up to keep a tally of the amount of money raised as the evening went on. And there on the counter were a hundred pairs of bright, clean skates. Several dozen skaters were already in the rink warming up.

Slowly, Elizabeth and Amy turned to the Unicorns, who were all grinning broadly. "I guess you think you made fools out of us," Elizabeth said sheepishly.

"I guess they did make us look pretty silly," Amy admitted.

"Were you in on this?" Elizabeth asked Jessica.

"Of course!" Jessica laughed. "You two were so sure we'd mess this up that we had to show you we could do it!"

Elizabeth glanced over at the sign-in booth, where a line of people had already formed. At this rate, by the end of the skate-a-thon, Elizabeth knew the Unicorns would have raised more than enough money for the new encyclopedia set.

Elizabeth shook her head. "I hate to admit it, but I think this is a perfect story for me to write about in the *Sweet Valley Tribune.*"

"Just make sure you spell my name right," Lila said triumphantly. "It's L-I-L-A."

"Lila, don't you think you're taking this a little too far?"

"All I asked is that you run and get me a soda, Jessica," Lila said, sitting down in a chair. The skate-a-thon had been going for more than three hours. A hundred skaters had been gliding around and around in seemingly endless circles. "Watching all these people skate is making me thirsty."

"Well, go get your own soda," Jessica replied grumpily.

"Why? Don't you think you'll be able to *see* well enough to find the refreshment stand?" Lila asked sweetly.

"Sh!" Jessica glanced around quickly, but no one was close enough to have overheard Lila's remark. She gave Lila a dirty look, but Lila just smiled up at her innocently. "All right, Lila," Jessica snapped. "I'll get your soda, but—"

"—and a pack of corn chips, too," Lila interrupted. "I'm getting hungry."

Jessica bought the soda and corn chips and was heading back to give them to Lila when she passed Elizabeth.

"Hi, Jess. Hungry?"

"Not exactly," Jessica answered, gritting her teeth. "This is for Lila."

"Lila?"

"Yes, Lila!" Jessica cried. "She knows all about my"—she paused to look around carefully, then whispered—"glasses."

"What's she doing, blackmailing you?" Elizabeth asked.

"How did you guess?"

"I know Lila," Elizabeth said.

"Well, she hasn't exactly threatened to tell," Jessica explained. "But if I don't do whatever she says, I know she will."

"But Jess, this can't go on forever," Elizabeth pointed out.

"I know that. Lila will never be able to keep the secret for long, but I'm hoping that she'll at least keep her mouth shut till after my date with Aaron."

"Jessica, this is ridiculous," Elizabeth said flatly. "You're letting Lila push you around. And you're risking getting into trouble with Mom and Dad for no reason except your silly vanity!"

"What do you mean, *silly*?" Jessica said. "If I'm seen wearing—" She broke off as she noticed Ellen coming toward them. "So, Elizabeth," she continued loudly, "do you have enough information about the Unicorns for your article?"

"What?" Elizabeth seemed confused until she too noticed Ellen approaching. "Oh—right. Yes. Yes, I have plenty of information for my article. But I have to go check on how much money has been raised so far. Um, bye, Jess. And good luck!"

"Good luck?" Ellen asked Jessica. "Good luck for what?"

"Just good luck, Ellen!" Jessica said angrily. "Can't my own sister wish me good luck without me getting cross-examined?"

"Why are you in such a bad mood?" Ellen demanded. "Everything is going great!"

"For you, maybe," Jessica said darkly.

"Well, come and see Belinda's baby brother. That will put you in a better mood."

"Belinda's baby brother?" Jessica asked.

Ellen nodded. "Belinda's parents came by to see the skate-a-thon, and they brought Billy along. He's so cute!"

"I'd like to go, but first I have to give Lila this stuff," Jessica said.

"Lila's over looking at the baby, too. Come on."

Jessica followed Ellen to the far end of the stands, where a crowd of girls had formed around the baby.

"Here!" Jessica said, roughly shoving the drink and chips into Lila's hands.

"Thank you so much," Lila said sweetly. "It was awfully nice of you."

"Isn't Billy adorable?" Elizabeth asked, joining up with Jessica again. "He makes me wish we had a little brother."

"Well, maybe a little sister," Jessica replied. "One brother is plenty."

"He is kinda cute, isn't he?" A voice asked from behind them.

Jessica spun around. "Aaron! Hi! How long have you been here?"

"I just got here." He smiled at Jessica. "It looks like fun. I—I guess you've already skated so much, you're probably sick of it by now."

"Actually, I haven't skated once," Jessica said. "The only pledges I got were from my parents, and I'm sure they'll contribute the money whether I skate or not. After all, I'm one of the organizers and I *do* have certain responsibilities."

"Then I guess you're probably too busy to go skating with me now," Aaron said shyly.

"No, I'm all finished with my work," Jessica

answered quickly. "I mean—I guess the others can manage without me for a while."

Aaron and Jessica selected skates and put them on in a corner of the rink near the side exit. Jessica tucked her shoes inside her backpack next to her glasses, making sure not to let Aaron see the telltale blue leather eyeglass case.

"Come on!" she cried. Jessica headed for the rink and glided out easily into the crowd of skaters. She was a good skater, but Aaron seemed a little uncertain at first.

"I don't exactly skate much," he admitted, laughing at his own awkwardness. But after a few minutes, he became more confident and was able to keep up with Jessica.

They'd been skating for half an hour when suddenly, out of the corner of her eye, Jessica saw two very familiar-looking people join the crowd of onlookers. She had to squint to be sure she was right. Unfortunately, she was.

Her parents were there, and she was trapped!

It was only a matter of time before her mother and father would notice that she wasn't wearing her glasses. Her only hope was to escape out the side exit. But she couldn't turn around and skate against the heavy flow of skaters. She would have to pass directly in front of her parents in order to reach her backpack and escape!

Then an idea struck her. Lois Waller was skating ahead of her. *Lois Waller wore glasses*. Without a moment's hesitation, Jessica put on a sudden burst of speed and plowed directly into Lois.

Both girls went sprawling, and Lois's glasses popped off her face and went skittering across the floor. In an instant Jessica was back up on her skates. She swooped down on Lois's glasses and snatched them up.

"My glasses!" Lois wailed.

"I have them," Jessica called. "I'll skate all the way around and bring them back to you. Wait there!"

Before Lois could answer, Jessica sped off and caught up with Aaron, who had been unable to stop. "Are you OK?" he asked.

"Sure!" Jessica said brightly. "It was just a little accident. I rescued Lois's glasses." She showed him the glasses she was holding as they rounded the turn. The crowd of skaters still hid them from her parents' view, but in a moment she knew they would be passing right in front of them.

"I wonder how things look through glasses?" Jessica said aloud. "Maybe I'll try these on and see." She settled the glasses onto her nose just as they swung past her parents, who were sitting several feet back from the edge of the rink. Jessica smiled and waved. *Jessica*, she told herself, *you're a genius!*

As soon as they were safely past her parents, Jessica turned to Aaron. "That was really fun, Aaron, but I have to go. Right now. Will you give these back to Lois for me?"

"Sure, Jessica," Aaron said, looking a little confused.

"See you Sunday, Aaron!" Jessica called over her shoulder as she dashed toward the side exit. She found her backpack right where she had left it. Quickly, she knelt down to untie her skates and put on her shoes. In a moment she would be out the door into the parking lot, where she could find her parents' car and wait safely in the back seat until they came out. They would never know that she hadn't been wearing her glasses.

Jessica could hardly believe she had gotten away with it. Then she noticed two pairs of legs standing right in front of her. Slowly, she raised her head and looked up.

"Nice try, Jessica," her father said grimly.

Ten

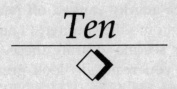

"Where's Jessica, Elizabeth?" Mrs. Wakefield asked on Saturday morning. "We've all been up for hours, but nobody's seen her."

"I figured she was sleeping late," Elizabeth replied. "I'll go see if she's awake yet."

Elizabeth knocked on Jessica's door but got no answer. "Jess?" Elizabeth opened the door a few inches and poked her head inside. "Are you awake?"

"I'm in here," Jessica called from the bathroom that connected the twins' bedrooms.

Elizabeth found her twin, still in her pajamas, standing in front of the mirror. She was wearing her glasses.

"Mom wondered where you were," Elizabeth said, leaning against the doorframe.

"From now on, I'll be easy to find. I'm staying in my room for the rest of my life. Mom and Dad may be able to force me to wear these stupid things, but that doesn't mean I have to go out in them." Jessica angrily yanked off her glasses and dropped them onto the counter. "I am never, ever letting *anyone* see me wearing these."

"But Jess, you really do look great in them," Elizabeth protested.

Jessica shook her head and pushed past Elizabeth into her bedroom. "I don't need your pity, Elizabeth," she said proudly. She collapsed onto her bed and crawled under the covers.

"I wish I could make you believe me," Elizabeth said.

"Well, you can't," Jessica retorted, "so don't bother trying."

"Are you going to stay in here all day?" Elizabeth asked.

Jessica pulled the covers up around her chin and nodded. "If anyone phones, tell them I'm not accepting any calls."

"Whatever you say." Elizabeth closed the door and headed back downstairs.

"Bad news, Mom and Dad," she announced

grimly when she got to the den. "Jessica says she's never coming out of her room again."

"Bad news?" Steven exclaimed. "That's great news!"

"Does this have anything to do with our discussion last night about her glasses?" Mr. Wakefield asked.

Elizabeth sat down on the couch next to Steven. "Yes. She says she doesn't want anyone to ever see her wearing them."

Mrs. Wakefield sighed. "Maybe we should have a talk with her, Ned."

"This is just a stage," Mr. Wakefield assured her. "Jessica will snap out of it."

"I'm not so sure, Dad," Elizabeth warned. "She's not even taking phone calls."

Steven whistled. "This is serious!"

Mr. Wakefield put aside the newspaper he was reading. "Why don't we all go upstairs and see if we can talk some sense into Jessica?"

"I've been trying to do that ever since she was born," Steven remarked.

"Steven, if you're not going to be helpful, you can stay downstairs," Mrs. Wakefield admonished.

"It might not hurt to have a boy's opinion, Steven," Elizabeth suggested. "Just tell Jess how great you think her glasses look."

Steven rolled his eyes. *"Girls,"* he said disgustedly.

With Elizabeth leading the way, the family headed upstairs and paused outside the door to Jessica's bedroom.

"Jessica?" Mr. Wakefield called, knocking gently. "Can we come in?"

"I really don't feel like talking, Dad," Jessica responded.

"Honey, you can't just lock yourself in your room forever," Mrs. Wakefield said.

"Why not?" Jessica asked.

"Because—" Mrs. Wakefield looked at the others helplessly. "Because we'll miss you, that's why. And so will all your friends."

"I won't have any friends when they see what a nerd I've become."

Mrs. Wakefield tapped Steven on the shoulder. "Your turn," she whispered.

"Me?" Steven shrugged helplessly. "What should I say?"

Elizabeth poked him in the ribs. "Say something nice, Steven. It won't kill you."

Steven stepped closer to the door. "Jess?" he called.

"Go away, Steven," Jessica replied.

"I just wanted to tell you that you're all wrong about your glasses," Steven began.

He paused, and Elizabeth gave him a nod of encouragement.

"I mean, they don't make you look any worse than usual," he added.

Elizabeth kicked her brother in the shin.

"Ouch!" Steven cried.

"Thanks, Elizabeth," Jessica called from behind the door.

"Jess, please come out," Elizabeth urged. "I thought maybe we could go shopping at the mall this afternoon."

"Wouldn't you like a new pair of shoes to go with your new outfit from Kendall's?" Mrs. Wakefield added. "Don't forget, you have a date tomorrow."

Elizabeth looked at her mother and crossed her fingers. If a shopping bribe didn't work on Jessica, nothing would.

"I don't need new shoes," Jessica announced loudly. "I'm not going out with Aaron."

"This really *is* serious!" Elizabeth murmured. She had only twenty-four hours before Jessica's date with Aaron to change her sister's mind. And it wasn't going to be easy!

Elizabeth put the finishing touches on a peanut butter and banana sandwich and placed it on a plate.

"Is that for Jessica?" Mrs. Wakefield asked.

Elizabeth nodded. "It's all part of Plan A."

"And what exactly is Plan A?"

"It's my plan to convince Jessica she doesn't really want to spend the rest of her life in her room."

"Well, I hope it works better than our last attempt did," Mrs. Wakefield said with a wry smile.

"It will," Elizabeth replied confidently. "I have a secret weapon. I'm going to make Jessica jealous!"

When she got to Jessica's room, Elizabeth knocked on the door. "Jess? It's me. I brought you a sandwich."

"Are you alone?" Jessica asked.

"Yes," Elizabeth said.

"Then come on in."

Jessica was sitting up in bed reading the latest copy of *Smash!* "Thanks, Elizabeth," she said, reaching eagerly for the plate. "I was starving."

"You could come down, you know," Elizabeth pointed out.

"No way. What if someone shows up at the door? What if Aaron comes by for some reason?"

Elizabeth sat down on the edge of Jessica's bed. "You know, I've been thinking, Jess," she began in her most innocent voice. "Aaron is awfully cute. And he's really nice, too."

Jessica looked up in surprise as she swallowed a bite of her sandwich. "I thought you liked Todd."

"I do," Elizabeth replied, twirling a lock of hair around her finger. "But that doesn't mean I can't like Aaron, too."

Jessica shrugged. "I suppose not." She picked up her magazine and began to thumb through the pages.

Elizabeth frowned. Jessica wasn't taking the bait very well. She was going to have to ham it up a little more, the way Jessica would. "I've been thinking," she said as casually as she could, "that it's a shame to waste a perfectly good Lakers ticket. And since you don't want to go to the game . . ." Elizabeth paused, waiting to see if Jessica seemed annoyed yet. "Jess?"

"Did you say something, Elizabeth?"

"I was wondering if *I* should go with Aaron. That is, because you don't want to," Elizabeth said.

"Sure." Jessica took another bite of her sandwich. "Go ahead. Or maybe Steven should go. He's dying to see the Lakers play."

Elizabeth couldn't believe her ears. Jessica wasn't jealous. She wasn't even *interested*!

"Thanks for the sandwich, Elizabeth," Jessica said.

Elizabeth jumped off the bed and headed for the door. *So much for Plan A*, she thought in frustration. *Too bad I have no idea what Plan B is!*

Later that afternoon, Elizabeth came up with Plan B. First she made sure Jessica's door was open a crack. Then she went to the telephone in the upstairs hallway and pretended to dial Amy's phone number.

"Amy?" Elizabeth said loudly, trying to ignore the dial tone buzzing in her ear. "Do you have a minute? I've just got to talk to someone about Aaron Dallas!"

Elizabeth glanced over her shoulder at Jessica's door. To her relief, she could see her sister peering through the crack.

"The thing is, I'm so jealous of Jessica," Elizabeth continued. "I'd give anything to be able to go out with Aaron." She paused for effect. "I know he likes Jessica, but I can't help the way I feel! He's so cute, Amy."

Elizabeth paused again, pretending to let Amy talk. *I'm really pretty good at this*, she thought with satisfaction. *Jessica's not the only actress in the family!* She peeked over her shoulder to be sure her sister was still listening.

Jessica was gone!

Elizabeth nearly dropped the phone. Maybe she wasn't such a wonderful actress after all. She pretended to talk about Aaron for a few more minutes, just in case Jessica came back. Finally, she gave up. "OK, Amy," she muttered. "Talk to you later."

She hung up the phone and peeked inside Jessica's open door. Her sister was lying on her bed, sound asleep.

So much for Plan B.

Jessica pretended to sleep until Elizabeth had left the doorway. *Nice try, Elizabeth,* she thought. But Elizabeth would never really go out with Aaron. Her sister was just trying to make her jealous. Elizabeth had never been a very good actress.

Jessica pulled the pillow over her head. It was awfully boring being stuck in her room. But then, she supposed that boredom was normal for nerds. She might as well get used to it. Her days of popularity and fun were over. On Monday she would walk into school wearing her glasses, and there would be howls of laughter from everyone.

She would just have to handle it with dignity. First, she would resign as a member of the Unicorns. That would be better than getting kicked out. Then she would quit the Boosters. And then she would just have to start hanging around with nerds and geeks. How hard could that be? She would just have to wear unfashionable clothes, no makeup, and study all the time.

Jessica yawned widely. "I might as well sleep. It's not as if I have anything to stay awake for."

But she slept for only a few minutes. She woke with a heavy pressure on her face. Slowly, she struggled to sit up, and as she did, she caught sight of herself in the mirror. The pressure on her face was from a pair of glasses wider than her head! They were so huge that her entire face was hidden, all but her eyes, which were magnified until they were as big as apples!

Jessica jumped to her feet and tried to take the glasses off, but her mother suddenly appeared, wagging her finger in warning. "You have to keep them on!" her mother scolded.

Jessica tried to leave her bedroom, but the glasses were so huge, they wouldn't even fit through the door. She turned sideways and at last managed to slide out, but as soon as she did she was suddenly surrounded by all the Unicorns, laughing and pointing and calling her "geek"!

"I am *not* a geek!" Jessica cried. "I'm the most popular girl in school!"

"Oh, no, you're not!" Aaron Dallas said, appearing right in front of her. "You're the biggest nerd in school. And I don't go out with nerds!"

"I'm not a nerd! I'm not a nerd!" Jessica cried desperately.

"Nerd, nerd, nerd," the Unicorns chanted.

I hope this does it, Elizabeth thought. *I'm running out of ideas.* She pushed open Jessica's door and closed it loudly behind her.

Jessica's lids fluttered open. "Elizabeth?"

"Oh, did I wake you?" Elizabeth asked innocently. "I didn't expect you to be sleeping at two in the afternoon."

"I was taking a nap." Jessica shook her head in confusion. "And having a really horrible dream. I had to wear glasses, and I became a nerd!" Then she caught sight of the glasses sitting on her nightstand. "Oh, no! It wasn't just a dream! It was real!"

"Very funny, Jessica. I guess you wouldn't be interested in going to the mall with me?"

"I already told you no," Jessica said. "And after that dream, I'm more sure than ever!"

Elizabeth smiled sweetly. *It's time for Plan C*, she thought. "I was hoping you could help me pick out something for my date."

"Your date?" Jessica echoed, yawning. "What date?"

"With *Aaron*, silly. I figure if you're not going to go, someone might as well enjoy herself."

Jessica rolled over and pulled the covers over her head. "Have fun shopping."

Elizabeth slammed the door behind her. She knew her twin was stubborn, but this was ridiculous!

Still, she had taken Plan C this far. She wasn't about to quit now.

Elizabeth dashed downstairs. She found Mrs. Wakefield in the backyard, working in the garden. "Mom," she asked breathlessly, "can I have a ride to the mall? I have an idea, and I need you to help. It's *very* important!"

Eleven

◇

Jessica glanced at the digital clock on her nightstand, just in time to see it change from ten after
five to eleven after five. Four minutes later than
the last time she had checked.

She picked up her magazine and threw it across
the room. She had read every article in it twice.
She now knew Donny Diamond's favorite food
(pizza), Kent Kellerman's secret dream (to play
professional football), and Melody Power's pet
peeve (people who are late).

Now that she thought about it, Elizabeth was
awfully late herself. Her twin had been at the mall
for nearly three hours now. She certainly was taking her time.

Jessica climbed back into bed. Maybe she would try to take another nap. It was too bad she wasn't the least bit sleepy. Besides, there was always the chance she'd have another horrible dream.

Downstairs, the front door slammed, and a moment later Jessica heard footsteps on the stairway.

"Jessica?" Elizabeth called from the hallway. "May I come in? I have a surprise for you."

"Sure," Jessica answered. "What did you—" She stopped in midsentence when Elizabeth burst into the room. *"Elizabeth?"* she gasped. "Is that *you?"*

"What do you think?" Elizabeth asked, spinning around. She was wearing a gorgeous new purple sweater.

And Elizabeth was wearing glasses!

"What are those?" Jessica asked, blinking in amazement.

"My new glasses." Elizabeth laughed. "Isn't it nice to be identical again?"

"Are they real?"

Elizabeth shook her head. "The lenses are just plain glass."

"But . . . you look—"

"I look *what?"* Elizabeth wanted to know.

"You look *cute!"*

Elizabeth nodded with satisfaction. "And if I look cute, then you must look—"

"—incredible!" Jessica exclaimed, finishing her sister's sentence for her.

"That's what I've been trying to tell you!" Elizabeth said. "*Now* do you believe me?"

Jessica looked closely at her twin. "I hate to admit it, but you were right all along."

"Then Plan C is a success!" Elizabeth announced triumphantly.

"Plan C?" Jessica looked puzzled.

"It's a long story. The point is, you've finally realized how great you look in glasses!"

Jessica frowned. "Well, not exactly, Elizabeth. What I've realized is how great *you* look in glasses."

"But—"

"It's really too bad you're not the one with bad eyes," Jessica continued. "On you, glasses look perfect."

"But we're *twins*!" Elizabeth exclaimed in frustration.

Jessica shook her head. "Glasses are perfect for your image, Elizabeth. You're a great student. You love to read. You're the editor of the school paper. You *should* be wearing glasses." She sighed. "But I'm a Unicorn. A Booster. And of course, I'm popular. Glasses just don't fit with my image."

"No matter how cute you look?" Elizabeth argued.

"You may think I look cute, and I may think I look cute, but what about other people? People like Aaron? He wanted to go out with a popular Unicorn, not the kind of girl who wears glasses."

"But how do you know that for sure?" Elizabeth demanded.

"I just do." Jessica patted her twin on the back. "Thanks for trying, though, Elizabeth." She pointed to Elizabeth's glasses and smiled. "I know those are fake, but maybe you should start wearing them, anyway. You *do* look awfully cute."

Elizabeth trudged out to the hallway, looking very dejected. Mrs. Wakefield was waiting at the head of the stairs. "What happened?" she asked eagerly.

"Jessica finally realized we were right about glasses," Elizabeth said sadly.

"That's wonderful!" Mrs. Wakefield beamed.

"She thinks they look adorable—on *me*," she added, and sighed.

"Do you think I should call Aaron's parents?" Mrs. Wakefield asked Elizabeth on Sunday morning. She came into Elizabeth's room and sat down on the edge of her bed.

Elizabeth looked up from the *Tribune* article

she'd been working on. "Let's give Jess a little more time," she suggested. "She still might change her mind."

"Your father and I are going over to the Steele's this afternoon," Mrs. Wakefield said.

"Are they your friends with the five-year-old daughter?"

"Chrissy," Mrs. Wakefield responded. "You should see her, Elizabeth. She's just adorable." She smiled wistfully. "Almost as cute as you and Jessica were at that age." She glanced at her watch. "Anyway, we'll be leaving soon."

"I'll call Aaron if Jessica doesn't change her mind soon," Elizabeth promised.

"Thanks, honey." Mrs. Wakefield stood up. "I suppose we ought to make Jessica call him herself, but she's so miserable, I'd hate to make things any worse."

"I know," Elizabeth said anxiously. "I've never seen Jess so unhappy. And the frustrating thing is that it's all in her head! She doesn't *have* to be so miserable!"

"Give her time," Mrs. Wakefield advised. "By the way, how's the *Tribune* article coming?"

"Great. The skate-a-thon gave me plenty to write about," Elizabeth said.

"Well, good luck with it. We should be home around five. And don't forget to call Aaron, OK?"

Elizabeth let another hour pass before she decided to give Jessica one last try. She went to Jessica's room, where she found her sister sitting at her desk doing her math homework.

"You must be really bored," Elizabeth joked, "if you're doing your homework."

"Was there something you wanted, Elizabeth?" Jessica asked frostily.

"I don't suppose you've changed your mind about Aaron, have you?"

"Nope," Jessica said firmly.

"I guess I'll call him and cancel your date, then. What should I say?"

"Tell him I turned into a nerd," Jessica replied matter-of-factly.

"It's a waste of a good ticket," Elizabeth argued.

"Then why don't you go? I know you were just trying to make me jealous yesterday, pretending to call Amy and all, but someone might as well have a good time."

"You knew I was faking it?" Elizabeth asked indignantly.

"Of course," Jessica replied. "Don't ever go into acting, Lizzie. Anyway, why don't you go to the game? You already have that cute sweater you could wear."

"Maybe I just will!" Elizabeth shouted in frustration, slamming the door behind her.

It would teach Jessica a lesson if I did go, Elizabeth thought angrily as she stomped back to her room. She looked at the purple sweater and fake glasses lying on top of her dresser and sighed.

Suddenly, an irresistible idea hit her. An idea so perfect, so outrageous, she couldn't believe she hadn't thought of it sooner. She quickly reached for the sweater.

Plan D was about to go into effect.

Jessica crumpled up her answer sheet and tossed it onto the floor. There was no way she was going to be able to concentrate on math this afternoon. This afternoon she was supposed to have been on her very first date with Aaron, having the time of her life. Instead, she was locked up in her room with her math book, staring at long columns of numbers until they blurred together on the page.

Jessica glanced at her clock. It was one o'clock, the time when her date was supposed to have started. She wondered what excuse Elizabeth had come up with. She hoped Aaron wouldn't be too disappointed.

Outside, a car door slammed. A moment later, Jessica heard the doorbell ring. *It's probably one of Steven's friends*, Jessica thought. She reached for a fresh sheet of paper and started to add the same column of numbers for the third time.

She could hear voices downstairs now. One of them, she was pretty sure, was Steven's. The other was a familiar boy's voice. A *very* familiar voice!

Jessica dropped her pencil and dashed to her bedroom door. It was Aaron! She was sure of it! But why was he here? Hadn't Elizabeth canceled their date?

Jessica clenched her fists together. Her twin wasn't actually going to the game, was she? Didn't she know Jessica hadn't been serious about Elizabeth taking her place?

Cautiously, Jessica eased open her door and tiptoed to the edge of the stairway. She had a clear view of the hallway where their visitor was talking to Steven.

It was Aaron, all right. He was wearing a Lakers T-shirt and what looked like a new pair of jeans.

Just then, Elizabeth appeared in the hallway. She was wearing the purple sweater she had bought yesterday at the mall. But there was something strange about the way Elizabeth looked. She was wearing her hair in long, loose waves, just the way Jessica always did. And she had a little makeup on, too, exactly the way Jessica wore it.

She's pretending to be me! Jessica thought with a sudden surge of anger.

But that wasn't the real surprise. Jessica squinted, blinked her eyes, and looked again to be certain she wasn't seeing things.

Elizabeth was wearing her fake glasses!

"Hi, Aaron!" Elizabeth said in a sickeningly sweet voice that made Jessica's blood boil.

"Jessica!" Aaron exclaimed. "You look—you look *great!* When did you get glasses?"

"The other day," Elizabeth said lightly, still doing her Jessica imitation. "Do you like them?"

"They're terrific! You look very , um . . . sophisticated," Aaron replied bashfully.

"Why, thanks, Aaron," Elizabeth said, batting her eyes. "I like them, too. But I only have to wear them for a couple of months." She reached for his arm. "Would you mind waiting in the den? I just need to go upstairs and get my purse."

As soon as Aaron was out of earshot, Steven leaned close to Elizabeth and inspected her carefully. "Just a minute," he whispered. "You're not Jessica, are you?"

Elizabeth giggled. "I'll never tell!"

Jessica leaned against the wall in the upstairs hallway. She was stunned. *Aaron liked her glasses!* Well, actually, he liked Elizabeth's fake glasses, but that meant he would like her real ones just as well!

But now *Elizabeth* was going out on *her* date! She couldn't believe that Elizabeth would do this to her. As Elizabeth passed by, Jessica reached out, grabbed her twin, and pulled her into her room.

"Who do you think you are, trying to go out on *my* date!" Jessica demanded furiously.

Elizabeth shrugged. "I thought you weren't interested."

"Of course I'm interested! Why wouldn't I be interested?"

"Because Aaron would see you in your glasses and think you were a nerd," Elizabeth explained reasonably.

"Aaron thought you were me, and he liked you in your glasses, so he's sure to like me in my glasses even more!"

Elizabeth laughed. "Exactly, Jessica."

"Besides, you don't even care much about basketball." Jessica looked sheepishly at her sister. "I guess I've been acting kind of stupid, haven't I?"

"The only stupid thing will be if you don't go out with Aaron. Now, hurry! We've got to turn you into Jessica!"

Quickly, the two girls exchanged clothes. "You

know, Elizabeth, you're pretty amazing," Jessica said.

"That makes two of us!" Elizabeth laughed.

A few minutes later, Jessica stepped into the den, wearing a radiant smile—and her own glasses.

"Weren't you wearing a different pair of glasses a minute ago?" Aaron asked as they headed into the hallway.

Jessica winked at Elizabeth, who was waiting by the front door. "A different pair? Why, no, Aaron. Maybe you should have your eyes checked!"

Twelve

◇

Jessica looked up at the huge stadium scoreboard and clapped her hands together happily. "Fifty-four to fifty at the half!" she exclaimed to Aaron. "What a great game!"

Aaron grinned. "It has been great, hasn't it? I'm really glad you could come, Jessica."

"I almost couldn't make it," she admitted.

"I'm sure glad you did," Aaron said. "Who would I have gotten to explain the Lakers' defensive strategy to me?"

Jessica giggled. "How about Bruce or Jake?"

Aaron shook his head. "I'm having more fun with you."

Jessica blushed. *Thank goodness Elizabeth talked me into coming today*, she thought gratefully. How

could she possibly have been silly enough to think
her glasses would make a difference to Aaron?

"You mind if I give you a compliment, Jess?"
Aaron asked softly.

"Who, me?" Jessica laughed. *Let me guess*, she
thought. *He likes my new sweater*.

"This is the most fun I've ever had at a basketball game. And you know why?" Aaron stared off
at the empty basketball court. "Because you know
so much about the game."

Jessica adjusted her glasses and smiled with satisfaction. Maybe she'd been wrong about her
image, after all. There was nothing wrong with
having brains *and* beauty!

"Listen to this!" Jessica exclaimed as the Unicorns gathered around the Unicorner at lunchtime
on Wednesday. After she cleaned her glasses and
slipped them on, she opened a copy of the *Sweet
Valley Tribune*.

"Hurry, Jessica!" Janet urged. "I can't stand the
suspense!"

" 'Students Who Make a Difference,' by Elizabeth Wakefield," Jessica read proudly. She cleared
her throat and continued. " 'The Friday night skate-
a-thon, sponsored by a group of sixth graders who
call themselves "Unicorns," raised enough money
to purchase a new encyclopedia set for the Sweet

Valley Middle School library. While Unicorns may be rare, this hard-working group proved that generosity is not.' "

"What do you think?" Elizabeth asked as she and Amy walked over to join the group.

"Elizabeth! It's wonderful!" Jessica cried.

"We're famous," Lila added. "I'm going to be sure my dad buys a hundred copies of this paper."

"Look out, Jess," Ellen whispered. "Here comes your true love."

Jessica waved to Aaron.

"If I·have to hear about your date one more time—' Lila stopped herself short and smiled at Aaron when he reached the Unicorner.

"I just wanted to see if you'd like to go to another Lakers game with me next weekend," Aaron said to Jessica. "My dad got an extra ticket just in case you wanted to come."

"Great!" Jessica said excitedly.

"*Another* date?" Lila groaned.

Aaron pointed to the *Tribune*. "What are you reading?"

"Elizabeth's article," Jessica replied proudly. "She's a Junior Journalist, you know."

"I guess this article proves once and for all that you were wrong about the Unicorns, Elizabeth," Janet said smugly.

"Well, I wouldn't go *that* far," Amy said. "By

the way, I heard this weird rumor that the Unicorns are planning to take the money left over from the skate-a-thon and install a full-length mirror in the sixth-grade girls' locker room!"

"What do the boys get?" Aaron demanded, pretending to be offended.

"You aren't serious, are you?" Elizabeth asked the group.

"Well, there wasn't enough money for curling irons," Janet said lamely.

"You mean it's true?" Amy howled. "Elizabeth! Get your notebook! What a great scoop for the *Tribune!*"

Elizabeth didn't answer. She was staring at the purple skirt and top that Lila was wearing. "Doesn't that outfit belong to Jessica?" Elizabeth asked, narrowing her eyes.

"She gave it to me," Lila replied defensively.

"But Jess!" Elizabeth cried. "You haven't even had a chance to wear it yet!"

"It's OK, Elizabeth," Jessica assured her. "It all worked out for the best." She smiled happily at Aaron.

"By the way, Jessica," Lila said. "I've been thinking. You know what would look great with this outfit?"

"What?"

"Your new glasses. I know I don't need them,

but do you think I could borrow them sometime? They would give me an *interesting* look," Lila said sweetly.

"I'm afraid not," Jessica said, winking at Elizabeth. "Glasses look good on me. After all, in addition to being pretty and popular, I'm also smart and sophisticated. But on you, Lila?" Jessica shook her head. "I'm afraid they would just make *you* look like a nerd!"

"Speaking of nerds, here comes Mandy Miller!" Ellen rolled her eyes. "I just wish she would leave us alone!"

"Yeah. Who does she think she is, trying to hang around with the Unicorns?" Janet said huffily.

Elizabeth frowned. "If I were you guys, I'd be thankful for Mandy's hard work. She *did* put up all the posters for the skate-a-thon. Maybe I should retract that bit in my article about generosity."

"Oh, please, Elizabeth," Jessica said. "It's not that Mandy isn't nice and all that. It's just that she's not special, like us."

"We'll see," Elizabeth said thoughtfully.

Is Mandy Miller special enough to be a Unicorn? Find out in Sweet Valley Twins #48, MANDY MILLER FIGHTS BACK.

A BANTAM SKYLARK BOOK

FRANCINE PASCAL'S

SWEET VALLEY

Twins AND FRIENDS.

Join Jessica and Elizabeth for
big adventure in exciting

SWEET VALLEY TWINS AND FRIENDS
SUPER EDITIONS

☐ #1: CLASS TRIP   15588-1/$3.50
☐ #2: HOLIDAY MISCHIEF   15641-1/$3.75
☐ #3: THE BIG CAMP SECRET   15707-8/$3.50
☐ #4: THE UNICORNS GO HAWAIIAN   15948-8/$3.75

☐ SWEET VALLEY TWINS SUPER SUMMER
   FUN BOOK by Laurie Pascal Wenk   15816-3/$3.50

Elizabeth shares her favorite summer projects
& Jessica gives you pointers on parties.
Plus: fashion tips, space to record your favorite summer
activities, quizzes, puzzles, a summer calendar, photo
album, scrapbook, address book & more!

SWEET VALLEY TWINS AND FRIENDS
CHILLERS

☐ #1: THE CHRISTMAS GHOST   15767-1/$3.50
☐ #2: THE GHOST IN THE GRAVEYARD   15801-5/$3.50
☐ #3: THE CARNIVAL GHOST   15859-7/$3.50
☐ #4: THE GHOST IN THE BELL TOWER   15893-7/$3.50

- -

Bantam Books, Dept. SVT6, 2451 S. Wolf Road, Des Plaines, IL 60018

Please send me the items I have checked above. I am enclosing $_____
(please add $2.50 to cover postage and handling). Send check or money
order, no cash or C.O.D.s please.

Mr/Ms _____

Address _____

City/State _____ Zip _____

SVT6-4/93

Please allow four to six weeks for delivery.
Prices and availability subject to change without notice.

A BANTAM SKYLARK BOOK

FRANCINE PASCAL'S

SWEET VALLEY
Twins AND FRIENDS.

Bantam Books, Dept. SVT5, 2451 S. Wolf Road, Des Plaines, IL 60018

Please send me the items I have checked above. I am enclosing $_____
(please add $2.50 to cover postage and handling). Send check or money
order, no cash or C.O.D.s please.

Mr/Ms _____

Address _____

City/State _____ Zip _____

SVT5-4/93

Please allow four to six weeks for delivery.
Prices and availability subject to change without notice.